Courage to Pray

Victoria Isabel Roberts

ISBN: 978-1-950281-02-2

Courage to Pray

Victoria Isabel Roberts

Berean Publications
P. O. Box 441116
Jacksonville, Florida 32222
Phone (904) 518-4220
www.BereanPublications.com

For Mr. Daryl Wells,

Your words inspired this story:

"What would it be like if there were a Daniel in today's world?"

CAST OF CHARACTERS

Daniel
Arthur
Sean
Matthew
Uncle Devon
Aunt Lisa
Neala (nee-yah-la)
Jane O'Malley
Roy Wilkins
Coach Mackenzie
Reganne (ree-gin)
Randy
Elliot
Pastor Moore

PROLOGUE

It began with the smallest of steps. Daniel slipped from the room and into the dim hallway. Flashing city lights played tag across his bare toes, jumping off the wall. He rubbed his bleary eyes, yawned, then wrinkled his nose. Why was he awake? It was too dark, and Mommy wasn't humming her morning song. His eyes widened as a new sound filled his ears. *The noise! What was it?*

He walked across the hallway toward the sound. His exploration ended at the door of his parent's bedroom. A small crack in the doorframe invited him to come closer. Pressing chubby fingers against the white wood, he pushed the door open.

The room was lit by candles and smelled like the white frosting he liked to lick off cupcakes. He approached the bed. The comfy place was cast in shadows by the candlelight. On the right side of the bed, his mother sat on her knees, her face buried in the comforter. The noise rose again as his mother sniffled.

Daniel furrowed his brow. *Was this the noise?* But, Mommy didn't cry. He rubbed his eyes again and then shuffled slowly toward her. Maybe a hug and kiss would help. Those always made him feel better. With a determined nod, he walked over to his mother's side. He reached up on tiptoes, placing his chubby fingers over one of her fists.

"Mommy," he said, "are you sad?"

For a moment, she didn't answer but unwound her balled fist and intertwined her fingers with his. Her sobs lessened, and soon she was breathing normally again. Giving his fingers a little squeeze, she straightened and wiped her face with the back of her free hand. Then she turned to him. A hint of a smile covered her lips as she looked down at him.

"Hey, Danny Boy," she said, "Lord knows I needed you tonight."

He frowned. "Do you have a boo-boo?"

"Yes, I have a boo-boo." She caressed her son's fingers. "But it's on my heart."

He cocked his head. "Hugs help."

Daniel's mother laughed softly. She let go of his hand and spread out her arms. "Yes, hugs help."

He wrapped his arms around his mother's neck, and she drew him close against her. He giggled as she rose, lifting him off the ground so his feet dangled in mid-air. She settled on the edge of the bed, placing Daniel in her lap and moving his arms to encircle her waist. With his head against his mother's chest, he listened to her heartbeat.

"Mommy, why does your heart hurt?"

His mother tugged at the edge of his blue plaid pajamas. She sniffled. "Mommy just misses Daddy."

"Because the angels took him away?"

"Yes, because the angels took him away."

He grabbed her trembling hand. "But Mommy, you said that he went to a beautiful place and that he is all better now."

"Yes, because he was sick…"

"Yeah, and shouldn't we be happy for him?"

"Oh, Danny Boy, I'm happy for him. I just hurt for me, that's all."

"Oh." He reached up and wiped away one of her tears with his little fingers. He frowned. "But will you feel better soon?"

"Yes, Danny, I will. These tears, they make me feel better. You make me feel better. Tears and prayer and you, and soon I'll be as good as new."

Daniel shifted as he peered up at his mother. "Prayer? What is prayer, Mommy?"

She caressed his cheek. "Prayer is talking to God, Danny Boy. I was just talking to Him when you came in."

"I don't see God. Was He is this room? Where is He now?"

"He's in my heart, where He's always been."

His eyes widened. "Did He make you cry?"

His mother pressed him closer. She laid her head on his and closed her eyes. "No. I cried because I was mad at God, and I had an argument with Him." She paused. "Sometimes, though, arguing with Him only helps me see how wrong I was and…and, that's why I cried…because I had forgotten God." She looked down at her son while cupping his small face with her hands and gazing into his eyes. "But, Danny Boy, He's never forgotten me; and, now I will try to talk to Him more. I will even teach you to talk to Him."

"By prayer?"

"Yes, by prayer."

Daniel glanced at the shadows playing outside the window. His daddy always helped him chase away the night's shadows. But he wasn't here now. God had taken him away. Daniel shivered and buried his face into the comfort of his mother's soft, lilac nightgown.

"Is prayer scary?" he asked.

There was a moment of silence before his mother answered. She ran her hands up and down his back. Then, she cleared her throat.

"No, Danny Boy, prayer is a safe place. Sometimes, in prayer, you fight with God's enemy called the Devil, but God is always there. He takes the load off your shoulders and wraps you in His love. In prayer…you have a Comforter…you find a Shelter for your life."

"Like when I'm in your arms?"

She smiled against his dark hair. "Yes, but God's arms are bigger and stronger. They hold the whole world."

Daniel and his mother sat still for a while. They clung to each other in the darkness, thinking of the only One Who could fill the empty space in the big bed next to them. This was the very same One from Whom his mother had been trying to run…the One Whom

11

Daniel had just discovered...the God Who promised to heal them. It felt good to know they were not alone.

Daniel peeked at the dark window in the corner again. The shadows remained, but between the shadows there was light. He sat up straighter. Maybe the God Who was with his father could chase away the shadows.

"Mommy," he said, "I want to pray, right now. Can I?"

Daniel's mother closed her eyes. She smiled as another tear escaped, falling against his downy hair. Taking a deep breath, she released in a whisper, "Of course."

"How?"

"Just close your eyes and speak to Him."

For a moment, Daniel remained silent. He closed his eyes, furrowed his brow, and waited.

Then his voice cut through the silence.

"Dear God, I'm Daniel."

CHAPTER 1
ALONE

They spoke words in low tones as if he couldn't hear them. *Alone. Orphan. No one else.*

Daniel burrowed into the hard plastic chair of the waiting room. The strong smell of chlorine burned his nose. He should be used to it by now. The taste that coated his tongue from the sterile environment was more familiar than the strangers in the next room. He closed his eyes against the torrent of thoughts bombarding him. One prominent thought rose above the rest. *Why?*

A hand rested on his shoulder. He looked up to find a familiar face smiling down at him. He straightened as she smiled, a sheen of tears on her face.

"I'm so sorry, Daniel. She meant a lot to all of us."

He felt as if he should answer, but his throat closed and a lump rose instead. He swallowed hard, nodding. The nurse squeezed his hand tightly before entering the room across the hall. The empty room.

Daniel watched from a distance as the nurses stripped the bed of its sheets. They moved the IV machine and sterilized every surface. Nothing remained of its former resident—not even her germs. She would no longer use this bed to watch soccer games with her son. She would no longer need that tray of hospital food. She would no longer close her eyes, resting against the pillows as he read comforting passages of Scripture.

He ran his hand over his face as his vision blurred. What would life be like now? For so long, this place had been his norm. For so long, he had fought beside his mother for her life. Now that it was over, he had to keep living...without her.

The door behind him opened. He sat straighter and blinked to clear the tears in his eyes. Uncle Devon stood before him, his arms crossed in front of his ample belly with his wife's hand tucked into the crook of his arm. He tried to smile, but his lips twisted instead. He cleared his throat.

"How are you feeling, Boy?"

Daniel opened his mouth then closed it. What could he say? He shrugged and lowered his eyes.

His uncle rubbed the back of his neck. "You'll be coming with us to Georgia now."

Daniel nodded. There was no need to respond. This wasn't a choice; it was his only option.

His uncle shifted back and forth in his tennis shoes. "Well, we best hit the road. We've got quite a drive ahead of us. Do you need anything else?"

Daniel looked one more time toward the empty room. Without a word, he walked across the hall and into the quiet space. The silence was almost unbearable. He scanned the various surfaces, trying to reconcile the emptiness. If he looked hard enough, he could still see her imprint on the bare mattress.

He felt a small tap on his shoulder and turned. The nurse who comforted him earlier stood behind him. In her hands she held a worn black book. She offered it to him. His eyes widened. How had he forgotten? With trembling hands, he reached for the Bible. He grasped it, the worn leather cool against his palm. He took a deep breath. Did he need anything else? Clearing his throat, he turned back to the doorway where his caretakers waited. "I'm ready."

As he walked down the hall, the whirring of hospital machines was the only reminder of the life he was leaving behind.

†

Beep. Beep. Beep.

Daniel jumped up and threw his covers aside. He took deep breaths, trying to slow the erratic beat of his heart. He looked around as his eyes adjusted to unfamiliar surroundings. The annoying pulse of the alarm clock filled his head. With a groan, he swung his legs to the right side of the bed. He shivered when his bare feet touched the cold wooden floor. Where was that alarm clock?

He felt his way around in the shadows, trying to follow the sound that continued to rise in volume. He found the alarm vibrating on top of the small corner desk. Finally, he clicked the off switch. The room fell silent.

Daniel sighed, leaning against the wall beside the desk. Another typical morning. He smiled.

"Good morning, God," he whispered. "This isn't going to be easy, is it?"

He shook his head. No point in pushing the snooze button now. He made his way to the bedside table, picking up his greatest treasure. He fingered the Bible as memories of the months with his mother filled his mind. He pressed it to his side and walked toward the door.

He looked down the hallway to his right. The door was still firmly shut with no light underneath. It was too early to wake the old couple, too early for him to start the bathwater that echoed throughout the house. There was only one thing that this time of day was good for. Solace.

Daniel exited his room toward the left. He tiptoed through the cozy living room. Behind him, the kitchen lamp gave him just enough light to avoid falling over the love seat and pile of books scattered across the carpet. He smiled, taking in the simplicity of his new environment. Would he ever be able to call it home? Turning his back to the kitchen, Daniel reached for the handles on the two sliding glass doors that led from the dining room to the stone slab patio. Noiselessly, he opened and closed them.

15

Inhaling deeply, he let the morning air fill his lungs. The fog clung to his skin with the scent of last night's rain. Dew graced the grass under his feet. This air was foreign to him, naturally raw with just a hint of city musk. Georgia was nothing like Detroit. He shivered, as recent memories stung his heart. His fingers tightened around the spine of his Bible.

He walked away from the patio into the yard. It spanned into acres of grass melding into woodland. He smiled. The trees created a haven around their house in the suburbs. He settled on a spot at the very edge of the woods where the grass was still thick, and the closest trees created a welcome canopy. He sighed as he sat Indian style on the damp ground. In the silence, he closed his eyes and lowered his head.

"God," he whispered, "why?"

The question hadn't left his tongue all summer. Now, as a new year approached, it remained in his life still. Why the emptiness and loneliness? He didn't want to be here alone, didn't want to be the only one listening to the birds above him. He opened his eyes, looking at the wide-open sky. His mother would have adored this place. She often planned to bring him to her brother's "countryside paradise," but something always got in the way—death, finances, and finally, the cancer. It had shaken the foundation of their home. When he closed his eyes, he could still hear the words she whispered when she was but a living corpse.

"I'm a fighter, Danny Boy," she had said, "We both are. This is not a death sentence. It is a challenge worthy of Job. We'll pull through together, you, me, and God."

"Like always," he'd responded. "Like always."

Yes, they had both fought the cursed disease like true warriors. Daniel and his mother had battled the depression, pain, bitterness, and awful fear of death with constant prayer and steadfast hope. Even now, Daniel could remember the worst night becoming bearable because of their growing faith; their constant cries to the Lord.

Through the New Year and into spring, they fought harder than ever before, hoping this nightmare would disappear and leave them alone. Instead, it materialized into reality, dragging Joy Stevens with it. And reality left Daniel Stevens an orphan.

He sighed. Now, the first morning of his senior year had come. He should be celebrating by eating blueberry pancakes with his mother. Instead, he was entering a new school…alone. His heart beat fearfully. *Alone.*

The word echoed in the corners of Daniel's frayed mind, threatening to undo his heart. He closed his eyes.

"God. Oh, God. She should have lived. I need…" he paused. What did he need? A mother? Well, that was certain.

He fingered the worn Bible that now rested on his knee. It was like carrying part of her with him. As he felt the tattered cover beneath his fingertips, he knew what he really needed. He swallowed hard.

"Okay God, I need You today more than ever. Please speak to me. I am…really…well, scared."

Daniel opened his eyes. He looked down, noticing the ribbon marker that stuck out from the bottom of the Bible. He flipped it open, desperate to remember where he and his mother had left off. He smiled as the pages came into focus. *Isaiah.* Along with Job, that book of the Bible was one they had read constantly their last year together. He read chapter 43 aloud. When he went through it once, his eyes fell back to a highlighted verse. It was verse two. As he read it again, his throat constricted, and he found he couldn't speak. Instead, he read it silently, letting the words soothe his soul.

When thou passest through the waters, I will be with thee; and through the rivers, they shall not overflow thee: when thou walkest through the fire, thou shalt not be burned; neither shall the flame kindle upon thee.

Daniel's eyes moved back to the statement after the first comma, *…I will be with thee…* He smiled. Tears of gratitude fell from his eyes. He could feel his Father standing before him, His all-encompassing presence wrapping around him. Daniel heard God whisper in his ear what he had just read.

I will be with thee.

He was not alone. He would never be alone. Daniel bowed his head. He smiled and surrendered to his morning prayers. Here, in his

Father's arms was, and always had been, a safe place. Soon, his aunt and uncle would call him back into this new world; but for now, he allowed himself to be comforted in a sweet hour of prayer.

CHAPTER 2
MASQUERADE

"Roy, please…"

"No, Jane! This is beyond ridiculous!"

Neala rolled her eyes as the sound of voices rose in the kitchen. After a night of peace, he had stopped by. Neala sighed. Good times never lasted forever. She stepped across the room and quietly closed the door, locking it for good measure. *I'm sooo not getting involved today. Jeez, give it a rest, Roy!*

She opened her closet and reached for a mini skirt and black tank. Considering her choice, she bit her lower lip, wondering if today would be one of the days her mother actually noticed. Most of the time, she could care less how Neala dressed. But…sometimes she noticed. Sometimes, she cared.

Settling on a metal stool in front of her dresser mirror, she brushed the tangles out of her long black hair. The comb passed through her tresses effortlessly, catching and straightening any tangles. As it settled around her shoulders, the voices in the kitchen grew louder. Glass shattered across tile floor. Jumping to her feet, she dropped the brush and ran toward the door. Her ears pressed against the cold white plaster. She waited for the scream. It never came. Instead, heavy footfalls sounded across the living room floor. Taking a deep breath, she walked back to the armoire but sat at the edge of her stool. *Just let him try to hit her again.*

She applied foundation on her olive skin, adding a heavy coat of liner and mascara to her eyes and lashes. How dare the worm treat her mother like that? How dare her mother let him? She closed her eyes. Her eyes moved to the small frame on her desk that held a dusty, faded picture. She fingered the frame. *Dad.* It was the last thing he'd handed to her before taking his military assignment. It was the last memory of "safe" she could remember. Her father had been a hero, a champion...

She sighed. He was nothing more than a distant memory now. Every one of her mother's boyfriends who trailed through their home trampled on all he'd fought for. Each one shattered her mother's future. They erased all the laughter and goodness from these walls.

The apartment door slammed shut, sending vibrations through the room and shaking the picture frame. Neala reached out to straighten it. She rushed to the window and peeked through the blinds. Roy stomped away across the crowded parking lot, frowning until he reached his Mustang and climbed inside. Stepping on the accelerator, he screeched away, his tires leaving dust to settle on the cars behind him.

The smell of burnt rubber floated through Neala's cracked window and she stepped away. *Finally.* She reached for the backpack at the end of her bed and pulled it over her shoulder. She made a quick inventory of her camouflage handbag. Everything was in place.

On her way out the door, Neala stopped in front of her full-length mirror. She frowned at her reflection, pulling her skirt down half an inch. She sighed. Then, she turned the knob of her door and stepped out into the hallway.

"Please notice, Mom," she whispered.

Neala threw her shoulders back and entered their tiny kitchen. Her mother stood over the trash can, getting rid of shards of glass from Roy's tirade. Neala cleared her throat. Her mother looked up, her face hidden behind thick red hair. She smiled, swept back her tresses, and straightened.

"My goodness, you're ready early this morning," she said.

Neala's heart sank. She looked over at the microwave so that her mother couldn't see the disappointment flashed across her face. The bright green numbers read: 7:15. She shrugged.

"I wanted to get there in time to hang out with Reganne and the gang."

Neala's mother shook her head. "I can't believe you're a senior."

She did a double take of her mother's eyes. Was there a gleam of pride shining in them? She lowered her eyes and caught sight of her mother's car keys. She had to change the subject. She reached for the keys and slid them away from her mother. Neala grinned.

"Which means I get to drive to school, right?"

Like a whiplash, her mom reached out and grabbed Neala's wrist. She raised her eyebrows, giving her a pointed look.

"Maybe you assume too much little missy. We only have one vehicle between us, and I need the car to get to work. Besides, you are not leaving this house without some breakfast."

Rolling her eyes, Neala dropped the keys into her mom's open palm and pulled away. She dragged her bags along with her as she approached the pantry. Her eyes scanned its contents, landing on a box of granola bars. She claimed the last one for herself. Moving to the refrigerator, she cast a backward glance toward her mother who stood at the kitchen counter drinking coffee.

"I do have to use my license sometime, you know?"

There was a moment of silence. Neala took that moment to reach for a bottle of strawberry milk. As she straightened and shut the door, her mother answered in a soft tone she hadn't used since she was a child.

"I know. I want to drive you to school, just for today. Okay?"

Neala leaned against the refrigerator door. She shrugged. "Fine, whatever. I don't care."

But I do.

She moved to open her granola bar, and then paused. She pushed away from the refrigerator.

"Tell you what, you drive while I eat."

Neala didn't need a response. She only had to walk to the door, knowing her mother would follow.

Stepping into the morning, she soaked up the autumn air. There was expectation drifting on the cool breeze, like the whole world was on the precipice of change. A shiver ran down her spine. Shaking it off, she walked toward her mother's '99 Volkswagen. It was just the excitement of a new year.

Neala jiggled the handle of the passenger door putting a little extra pressure on the right. In a matter of seconds, the passenger lock released. Grinning, she opened the door and threw her bags on the car's floorboard. She climbed inside, shut the door, and reached over to press on the car's horn. It sounded loud and clear. Then, Neala sat back, crossed her arms, and counted to five. On cue, her mother rushed out of their apartment, eyes wide. She glared at Neala as her panic melted into frustration. Shaking her head, she turned to lock the apartment door behind her.

Neala giggled. She reached for her granola bar. With a quick glance around the parking lot, she bowed her head and said grace. It was a rudimentary habit Neala had never stopped doing. It felt good to speak to Someone bigger than herself before her meals, even if He was so far away.

By the time Neala's mother got to the car, Neala already had begun eating her breakfast. Her mother climbed in beside her and started the car.

Hands on the wheel, she turned to give her a pointed look. "Young lady, I wish you would stop breaking into our car. Someone is bound to see you and take your lead one night. I have too much to worry about already."

Neala swallowed the last a bite of her granola bar and reached for the milk. "I didn't want to wait in the cold." She looked around at the shaking piece of machinery. "Besides, who would want any part of this junk car?"

Jane sighed. "It's transportation. Be grateful I'm not making you walk to school."

Neala strapped her seat belt over her shoulder as her mother backed out of the parking lot.

She cast her mother a sideways glance. "Why don't you ask Roy to help you get a new car? He has a pretty sweet ride. Besides, he's done enough damage to our house to owe us that much."

Jane gasped, taking the last speed bump too quickly. She gripped the wheel. "Neala! Watch your tongue. Roy is—"

"A pain!" she interjected before her mother could finish. "What was his problem this morning?"

"He just stopped by for a cup of coffee. He suffers from insomnia and was already in a bad mood. While he was telling me about his new job…"

"Let me guess, he got demoted."

"He's looking to get promoted. Anyway, I said something I shouldn't have." Jane shrugged. "It was a lover's quarrel. You're a grown woman now. You will understand someday."

Neala swallowed the bile that rose to her throat. Oh, she understood. She understood all too well what men wanted and expected.

She turned to glare at her mother. "No, I won't understand your lover's quarrels! I don't want to. I refuse to understand the kind of men you bring into our home so that they wreak havoc on our lives. Roy is no different. You're always saying there is nothing wrong with him, but you're wrong. Just like the dozen of men before him, everything is wrong with him. And you just stand by and take it!"

"Neala!"

"You deserve better. We both do. But there is nothing and no one better, is there? No, Mom. If that's the kind of relationship I have to look forward to, count me out. That is not love…"

"Enough, Neala! Life isn't all about fairytales and 'happily ever afters.' I have done what is necessary to live."

Jane shuddered. Her lower lip trembled. Neala could see tears welling up in her mother's eyes.

She looked away, swallowing back her own tears. Why did she always make her mother cry? She leaned against the windowpane, watching the world fly by. She wished, for just one second, that she could make life stop. This life was all she'd ever known, this life her mother gave her. And, what scared Neala the most was that she was running down the same track. She was sprinting one hundred miles per hour, and she had no idea how to stop.

For a moment, her mind wandered back to the lesson she had heard at youth night last week. Her mother wanted her to go to church so that she could "stay out of trouble." She didn't mind. She liked hearing about God, morals, and, last week, about purity. Neala had retained her purity so far, but this was a dark world. Outside of the church building, all her dreams of a pure life melted away. There was nothing for her to look forward to. She didn't know how to grasp the principles of Christian living. She was so afraid to.

Did God even care about her? Was she really that invisible? But of course she was. She was so small and God was so big. He needed to take care of the girls who had promise. What did He care about her inevitable destruction?

Neala's eyes flew open as excited chatter cut through the oppressive silence in the car. Her eyes took in the two-story building of Chancellor High. Fear twisted in her gut.

In the classroom, she would be able to lose herself in numbers, facts, and words. But, outside the classroom, with Reganne and the rest of the gang, she would not, could not, be Neala. She couldn't speak about her desires for chastity, her priorities, her standards, or her dreams. She definitely couldn't talk about God. No matter how many "standards" the administrator tried to uphold, God didn't belong here. The student body had willed it so.

She sat up straighter when her mom parked the car. She was dressed to fit in here; she could play the part. She would survive. She pushed open the car door and stepped onto the campus of Chancellor High.

"Have a good day," her mother said.

Neala felt an urge to lean over and hug her. She bit her lower lip. But if someone saw her…it was bad enough she was the only senior without her own car. She shook her head. Then, she grabbed her bags.

"Sure. Whatever. See ya." Neala shut the door.

Without a backward glance, she proceeded to the doors of the high school. She forced herself to take small steps, slowing her approach to what had become her theater. It was time to enter the masquerade.

CHAPTER 3
CUT

Roy slammed the car door shut, cursing under his breath when it squeaked and swung back toward him. He balled his hand into a fist. This piece of junk was almost not worth his time anymore. He took a deep breath, this time kicking the door with his left foot. It swung closed with a satisfying thump. He smirked. *Almost.*

Straightening his shoulders, he made his way across the staff parking lot. His eyes fell on the cars lined closest to the staff entrance of Chancellor High. He frowned. One day he'd be able to afford a shiny new ride. One day he'd be closer to the staff entrance. But not today. He reached for the glass door.

The back hallways of Chancellor High smelled like damp carpet and sawdust. Their budget allowed numerous updates for the student facilities but rarely provided for the staff. He coughed to clear the heavy film coating his lungs. He shook his head. If he were in charge…

"Good morning, Roy!"

He pasted a smile on his face while he looked over his shoulder as Principal Pierce approached him. His stomach churned. The old man's unassuming smile made him want to gag. He walked with confidence in his role, but he was dragging the school into the gutter. When the principal stopped before him, he accepted the man's offered hand. He squeezed a little too tightly. Principal Pierce simply smiled and continued on his way to the boardroom. Roy narrowed his eyes, following in the man's footsteps. The carpet quieted his steps, but his thoughts threw obscenities at the man's back.

He entered the boardroom after the principal. Numerous teachers and the remaining staff already filled their spaces at the long, mahogany table. Some loitered at a little donut and coffee stand in the back left corner. The sharp scent of coffee called to Roy, but he ignored it. His two cups from this morning would have to do. Besides, the sludge offered at this meeting was of little benefit to anyone. He moved to an empty spot at the center of the table. A stack of papers sat in front of him, outlining this month's agenda and budget. He folded his hands over the papers. It wasn't worth rifling through. It was always the same.

As Principal Pierce took his place at the head of the table, the rest of the staff hurried to fill the empty seats. Roy shifted, catching the eye of his assistant coach across the table. He nodded to him once. Then the principal's voice called their attention

"Let's open today's meeting with prayer."

The people in the room shifted as they bowed their heads. Roy rolled his eyes. He straightened in his seat. This was his favorite part of the meeting, not because he believed in this incessant need for prayer, but because he was now a head taller than everyone in the room, including the principal. He smirked, sweeping his eyes over the staff members. As the principal continued in prayer, asking assistance from his God, most simply dipped their heads and stared at the table. Some took out their phones, scrolling through their social media accounts. Others yawned and rested their heads on the table surface to take a short power nap. One or two joined the prayer time, but the rest simply pretended. Roy crossed his arms. *What hypocrites!*

He moved his eyes to the principal. Didn't he know what a fool he was making of himself? His leathery brow wrinkled as he concentrated on his prayer. Roy smirked. His meeting next week would be easier than he thought. He picked up the stack of papers before him. Flipping them over, he reached into the pocket of his sports shirt and grabbed his favorite pen. Its black, glossy surface felt secure against the palm of his hand. He wrote one word in the center top of the back page.

CUT

Roy grinned as he wrote out his plan for the future of this school. He followed the format familiar to him, drawing out his agenda in the form of a sports roster. Then he wrote down his changes. He slashed through each program that was old and unnecessary. There was a twinkle in his eye as he crossed out the one he hated most. As he wrote a few more notes on the bottom of the page, he heard Principal Pierce coming to the close of his prayer. He noiselessly flipped the pages back over. The morning meeting resumed.

As an hour of budgets and school event planning passed, Roy allowed his mind to wander. He might not count as much today, but soon he'd get all he ever wanted. Soon he'd have the pay and position he deserved. This was his year. It was time for change.

CHAPTER 4
CHANCELLOR HIGH

Daniel exhaled as his aunt and uncle drove away from the school. *That was such an awkward ride.* His guardians had attempted to start all sorts of conversations with no success. Daniel smiled. They would get past this gap. They were good people—more energetic and eccentric than he was used to—but good just the same.

Daniel turned to face Chancellor High School. It towered over him. The bright red bricks of the building stood out against the blue morning sky. Clouds drifted just above the highest floor, skimming the top but never touching it. *Untouchable.* He swallowed. Let the future hit him. With Christ, he was ready.

He hurried up the steps to the front door of the building. Three hundred students filled the halls of the upper and lower levels. Every single one came from a different background. Daniel paused inside the entrance, watching the flow of students moving back and forth. It reminded him of one of the big shopping malls in Detroit. Even at six feet, he felt like a small ant surrounded by an oblivious throng of humanity. Well, in God's record, ants were small in stature but big on wisdom. He shifted the backpack on his shoulder, smiling at the thought. Maybe being an ant was no big deal as long as he didn't get crushed.

Daniel walked past the school's main office and turned left. Last night, his aunt and uncle had provided him with a new student packet, courtesy of the administrator. In it, Daniel found directions to his locker, a class schedule, and a map of the school building and surrounding facilities—soccer field included. Taking another left past the bathrooms, Daniel found a hallway of lockers and classrooms. This was it. Now, to find locker number 107.

He walked down the hall, reading the numbers on each locker. A few of the students looked up at him in passing and, finding he was not familiar, quickly looked away. One guy glanced at him, rolled his eyes, and went back to texting. Daniel shifted his backpack again. Surely they hadn't labeled him as some freak already. He'd been here for only a few minutes.

Calm down, Daniel, you're jumping to conclusions.

He sighed when he finally found the locker. After entering the combination, he opened the door and found his textbooks inside. He lowered his backpack and lined his shelves with binders and folders. Then, he reached for his Bible. Aunt Lisa asked him to leave it at home, but he needed its comfort.

Shutting the locker door, he opened his Bible to reveal the poster sitting inside the front cover. The Crusaders.

Although the school administrator could not offer Bible classes, he did allow for a daily Bible study on campus. He scanned the poster's details. *Room 400.* Daniel looked around. *Where is that?* It wasn't on the school map. Daniel glanced at his wristwatch. He had ten minutes to make the 7:45 meeting. Should he just start walking or ask the nearest person?

"Are you okay? You look kind of lost."

Daniel turned. He couldn't help but smile. A few lockers down, a girl watched him, her arms crossed. She wasn't what he would call a "typical" answer to prayer, but she was an answer nonetheless. Daniel tried not to focus on her scantily dressed form but instead kept his eyes on her face. Jet black hair framed gentle features. Her eyes, hidden behind layers of makeup, reminded him of liquid silver. They were soft and inviting.

He cleared his throat. "Kind of? How about completely lost?"

She smiled and closed her locker. "You new around here?"

"This is my first day."

"Oooh. Well, welcome to the twilight zone. I'm Neala."

Daniel nodded. Out of habit, he offered her his right hand. "Nice to meet you. I'm Daniel."

She glanced at his hand, raised an eyebrow, then shook it. When they withdrew, there was a smirk on her face.

Daniel shifted. "What?"

She shook her head. "Your name just reminded me of one of my favorite songs: "Danny Boy." Has anyone ever called you that? I bet it would be pretty lame, huh?"

His next breath caught in his throat. He looked down for a second, regaining his composure. She had strummed the tightest chord of his heart.

When he met her eyes again, he forced a tight smile onto his lips. "My mom used to."

The teasing light in Neala's eyes melted into concern. "Used to?"

He looked away, catching sight of a tall blonde coming toward them. "It's a long story."

Neala glanced in the same direction. She moved closer, her voice a mere whisper and out of hearing range from the approaching girl.

"I'd like to hear it sometime."

"Neala!"

In response to the blonde girl's call, Neala stepped away from Daniel. She replaced her unguarded stance with a coquettish one. She smiled.

"Hey, Girl!" she called out.

The blonde arrived at Neala's side, breathless. She shook her head. "Where have you been? These heels are such a pain. Can you believe they put me on the second floor this year? I…"

Suddenly, the girl paused. Her eyes slid away from Neala and locked onto Daniel. Her perfectly plucked eyebrows raised an inch. She smiled demurely, reaching over to pat Neala's arm.

"Honey, you have Elliot. Don't keep the rest of the boys to yourself."

Daniel blushed. Under the tall blonde's gaze, he felt his heart beat double time. Unlike Neala, this girl's eyes were bold and alluring. His mind whirled as Proverbs spun within its depths. One in particular fell to the forefront. *Lust not after her beauty in thine heart; neither let her take thee with her eyelids.* Daniel took a deep breath. *Yes, God.*

With his thoughts under control, Daniel glanced back at Neala. She was blushing, and he saw discomfort in her eyes. Still, she smiled, a mask of coyness falling over her face.

"I would never be so selfish. Reganne, this is Daniel. He's new this year. Daniel, this is Reganne." Daniel managed a nod. Neala bit her lower lip as Reganne looked back at her. She looked at Daniel, panic in her gaze. "I was just helping him find..."

Daniel narrowed his eyes. For a second, he was at a loss for words. Why did he need directions? He raised his eyebrows. The poster! The Bible Study!

"Room 400," he blurted out. "Neala was giving me directions to The Crusaders. Do either of you attend?"

Reganne's flirtatious looks faded. Neala's eyes brightened, falling for the first time on the Bible in his hand. She veiled her interest with a blink of her eyes. A moment of silence followed. If they had been the only ones in the hallway, they could have heard each other's heartbeat.

Then, Reganne sneered. "Nope." she said.

Her nose upturned, she transferred her attention to her manicured nails.

Neala shot him an apologetic glance. "Um, we never attend, but feel free to help yourself. Room 400 is on the second floor. Take a right at the stairs and enter the library. Miss Mae will help you from there."

Daniel looked at his watch. He had five minutes. He opened his mouth to thank Neala but Reganne interrupted, turning her back toward him and waving.

"You may want to skedaddle," she said over her shoulder. "Elliot just spotted you cozying up with Neala, and he doesn't look happy."

He looked beyond Neala and noticed a tall jock coming toward them. He would like nothing better than to explain this misunderstanding, but the guy did not look like one who put much store in listening. He clutched his Bible. It was much too early to make enemies. Besides, his eyes fell on Neala; he may have just made a friend.

"Thanks," he said

Neala nodded, distracted by the footsteps behind her. She opened her locker and withdrew a sweater from its recesses. "Sure. You better go."

Daniel nodded. He turned reluctantly. Was there fear in her eyes? Who was this Elliot guy? Daniel took the steps two at a time. He would have to remember to pray for her. Something told him she might not have all of the strength that she feigned.

†

"Neala!"

She shivered at the sound of Elliot's voice behind her. She fastened the buttons of her sweater, ignoring Reganne's questioning eyes. Then, she turned to face Elliot. He barreled down the hallway, confidence in his steps and fire in his eyes. Those dark, burning eyes told his life story and never once did they leave Daniel's retreating form. He hadn't always been a bad guy, but high school had changed him. Fitting into a new crowd changed him.

Elliot stopped next to Reganne and Neala. He jutted his chin in the direction of the stairs. Neala followed his gaze in time to see Daniel take the last step.

"Who was that?" he demanded.

Neala bit her lower lip. "His name is Daniel. He's new this year and needed help getting around."

"New, huh?" Elliot took a few steps toward the stairs. "I should welcome him to Chancellor."

Neala's heart skipped a beat. She had seen that look in his eyes before. Quickly, she reached for Elliot's hand, intertwining their fingers together. She tugged him toward her. He looked back, his eyes telling her that she had his attention. Neala didn't like the feeling of his cold fingers around hers, but she kept them there anyway. She formed her glossed lips into a pout.

"Don't start trouble, Elliot. He's not worth it, honest."

"Yeah," Reganne piped in, "he's got nothing on you. He's heading over to The Crusaders. Figures, huh?"

Slowly, Elliot's firm mouth cracked with the hint of a smile. He squeezed Neala's hand. "Crusaders?" He winked at both of the girls. "I'll let others cause him trouble. He just asked for it."

They laughed and walked toward the front doors of the high school. They would meet the gang there, as they had every year. Neala cringed at the thought of others causing Daniel trouble. They stopped next to the group of guys labeled "friends," and Reganne began her incessant chatter. Neala hung back, her thoughts still on this odd newcomer.

Despite Reganne's lewd comments, he had carried himself far differently than Neala expected. He hadn't flirted back, not even once. And then there was that pain she'd sparked when she mentioned the song. It wasn't all encompassing though. There was a light behind that pain. It was as if he carried a secret. He knew of a remedy for that pain, any pain. Her thoughts whirled. Would he share the remedy? If he did, would anyone listen?

Reganne's voice cut through Neala's thoughts. All eyes fixed on her as her best friend told the gang about the morning's incident. The "new kid" was already being labeled as their next victim. She tried not to fidget. Finally, Reganne closed off the story.

"He is sooo out of her league," she said.

With that and a few snickers, the conversation turned to the latest celebrity news. Neala only half listened. The other half of her mind assessed those last words. She looked at Elliot's hand in hers, the bareness of her legs. She sighed, suddenly determined to never speak to Daniel again. Reganne was right. He was out of her league. But only for one reason.

I am way out of his.

CHAPTER 5
THE CRUSADERS

Daniel entered the library. His heart beat with the expectation of meeting new Christians. In the city, he had left behind numerous godly friends. All summer he had craved desperately for the companionship that distance made impossible. Would he find it here?

The library was equal in size to the cafeteria. Even this early, it was full. Unlike the hallway, this room exuded silence and peace. Daniel glanced around. Students of every personality sat in different chairs, entranced by a similar passion of books. But none of the groups seemed to be studying the Bible. He clutched his own copy, his eyes searching for the librarian's desk. He spotted it. What was the librarian's name? Ah, yes, Miss Mae.

Daniel approached the desk, his eyes falling on the librarian. She sat behind the oak desk, her eyes appropriately glued to a thick volume of Shakespeare. She looked younger than he expected. Her short, pleasantly plump form sat ensconced in a leather office chair. A piece of chestnut hair fell across her forehead and into her eyes. Daniel stopped before the desk. She didn't look up when his shadow fell over her. He waited a few moments before clearing his throat.

"Miss Mae?" he asked in a whispered tone.

With a start, she glanced up. She blushed, realizing she'd been caught shirking her duties. She set aside her book, straightened, and then met Daniel's eyes "Yes?"

Daniel laid the poster on her desk. "I'm looking for room 400. Neala said you could help me."

The librarian sighed. With one last longing look at her book, she nodded. "And so I can. Please follow me."

He smiled as she led him through aisles of literature and contemporary fiction. Books. There was a feeling of unity in a library, as if books strove to pull others out of the cruel world and into a common place of fantasy. He looked down at his Bible. Well, his favorite book strove for something better. This Book strove to pull others into a blessed eternity.

Miss Mae stopped before a door at the back of the library that was clearly labeled as 400.

"Here it is," she said.

Daniel smiled politely. "Thank you very much."

With a curt nod, Miss Mae scurried off. She escaped Daniel to lose herself in the drama of literature. Daniel turned the knob of Room 400 and entered the meeting place of The Crusaders.

The room was small and sparsely furnished. An L-shaped table encompassed the northern and eastern walls of the room while bare bookshelves lined up parallel to the door. Dust mites floated in the air around him. The whole room smelled of abandonment. The table was lined with numerous chairs, but only three were filled.

At the head of the table, a tall gangly boy addressed the others in the room. Next to him, a giant young man with green eyes and reddish-brown hair sat uncomfortably squeezed into a metal chair. Next to him, a short African-American boy fit into his chair with little difficulty, his legs crossed with a Bible lying across his knees. His arm muscles bulged as he shifted.

The floor creaked as Daniel stepped forward. All three turned to look at him, and a hush fell over the room. After a few moments, the tall boy spoke.

"May I help you?" he asked.

Daniel nodded. "I came to join The Crusaders. Am I in the right place?"

The leader's eyebrows shot up. Daniel tensed. Were they the kind of Christians who judged and rejected at first glance? The surprise in the leader's eyes turned to pure delight. Daniel felt himself breathe again as the leader stepped forward.

"You sure are!" he assured. He offered Daniel an outstretched hand. "My name is Arthur, but everyone calls me Art. That giant behind me is Matthew, and that little fellow is Sean. Please, make yourself comfortable."

He settled in a chair across from Sean, and introductions passed around the room. Finally, Art called the meeting to order. They opened in a word of prayer, and the Bible study began.

Art chose to delve into Proverbs 6. Daniel read along with them, his tongue rolling over the familiar words. It was so strange. Even here, so far from home, in the company of strangers, the words refreshed his heart.

When they read the verse about the ant's instruction for the sluggard, Daniel couldn't help but chuckle. He shared with the group his sentiments earlier this morning. Was it coincidence he had been reminded of his smallness again? They all laughed with him. Together, they agreed it was the Lord's perfect sense of humor and testified to the same amount of encouragement it lent. As the clock ticked down to the morning bell, they closed the session in prayer. Daniel stood. He was glad he had come. Despite the homeliness of the room, it suddenly felt like a foundation, a sanctuary. Daniel followed the group out the door and into the library. His heart beat with fervor. This was no ordinary place. God was here.

CHAPTER 6
ONE

The auditorium of Trinity Baptist Church looked the same since he took the pulpit.

Pastor Moore watched as adults came in from dropping off their children and took their places in their preferred pews. The drunkard came in from his midnight rounds, slumping in the back where he could sleep away the day. Members flipped through the bulletin, barely paying any attention to the piano piece that his wife had so carefully prepared. Teenagers whispered in low tones about the newest celebrity gossip, quieting and looking around whenever the youth pastor passed by. The ushers waited by the door. Visitors filled out information cards in the back. The eldest members sat solemnly in the noise around them. Everything was normal. Everything was the same.

Pastor Moore closed the door that led from his office into the sanctuary. He shuffled his notes. Yes, another sermon. Would anyone listen this time? He could count on his fingers the last time he'd actually seen someone in the audience move. The teenagers had their visitation every week, the bus ministry was overabundant, but the very core of the church was asleep.

He closed his eyes. Oh, how he wanted to see the hearts of the people moving beyond the scope of their comfort zone. How many revival meetings had he held in the last few years? The evangelists came and went with both fiery and gentle exhortations. Still, Trinity remained as it was, functioning without fire. He could not force revival on them. He could not force them to have a passion for Christ. If he could just find one with enough faith to move mountains, perhaps his own faith wouldn't flounder so easily.

He pressed the sermon notes against his heart. Closing his eyes, he lifted one more prayer to Heaven before the service.

"Lord, help me to be strong. Help me to hang on, even when your people just want to get through another service and be free for the rest of the day's activities. Please, send me one needy soul. One person concerned enough for Your sake to be filled with Your power. Lord, take me away from the pulpit, and fill the room with the Holy Spirit. Amen."

Pastor Moore opened his eyes just as his wife played the last keys of "Blessed Assurance." It was time to enter the sanctuary. As he approached the pulpit, the deacons closed the auditorium doors. Stragglers hurried to their seats. Pastor Moore looked out at the crowd. They looked up at him, waiting. It was always in this moment, before he spoke, that he felt the overwhelming love of God for this congregation. It was not his own love that got him up here, but the love of the One Who was looking out for the fallen at Trinity. God wanted him here for a purpose. He was going to do something big, in His time. With this thought, Pastor Moore opened the service in prayer.

At Trinity, if there was one thing the people did well, it was gathering their voices in song. Between the announcements and prayer requests, the entire building reverberated with hymns of praise. Pastor Moore allowed the songs to wash over him. Oh, how mighty was the God Who brought these people together under one roof.

By the time he stood to preach, the Spirit already had begun to move. He looked down at a group of teenage girls with their notepads and pens in hand to write notes. It was part of the youth group competition, but Pastor Moore hoped it would amount to more. He looked at the parents, grandparents, and visitors. As he led them to the morning passage of Amos 8:11 and 13, he prayed silently in his own heart for the ones for whom this sermon had been prepared. He read the Scripture verses aloud.

"Behold, the days come, saith the Lord God, that I will send a famine in the land, not a famine of bread, nor a thirst for water, but of hearing the words of the LORD:...In that day shall the fair virgins and young men faint for thirst."

That day, like he had every day before, Pastor Moore spent himself on the sermon. He spoke in loud tones and softer ones, heeding the Spirit. He allowed God to convey to the people that there was a spiritual famine in America. Those days had arrived. Amidst all the prosperity and wealth, the people's hearts had turned from God.

"The thing is, the most serious area affected by this famine is the church. Why are God's people starving so much? Because we do not study God's Word. We are so interested in following after the world's façade that we do not realize we are starving ourselves. In this light, how can the world see God? How can they drink of His living water if we do not drink of it ourselves? We are not only killing ourselves, but we are killing a nation and a world desperate for the water that gives eternal life."

People in the audience shifted. As sweat poured down Pastor Moore's brow and he trembled under the conviction of the Spirit, teenagers cleared their throats and wrote more quickly on the paper. The room was overflowing with God's Spirit. Pastor Moore could hear Him knocking on doors, begging to be let in.

"Friends, if you have never drunk of that living water, I would encourage you to do so today. If you have, but find yourself comfortable in a spiritual famine, come to the altar and renew yourself with Christ's living water. He will always fill your cup. Everyone bow your head and close your eyes. The altar is open. Let the Spirit lead you and come forward."

Pastor Moore's wife played soft strains of "I Surrender All." He continued to beckon the people to come. He waited, hoping for the Spirit to move. But the congregation remained seated. Once again, the altar was empty.

Bone weary, Pastor Moore prepared to bring the service to a close. Then, from the back of the church, he caught a slight movement. A young boy sitting next to an elderly couple rose to his feet. He walked toward the altar slowly and fell to his knees on the carpeted stairs. Pastor Moore couldn't speak. He stood there, watching as one young man did business with his Lord. When the boy moved back to his seat, he brought the service to a close. The moment he dismissed the people, a collective sigh moved through the congregation. Finally, it was lunchtime.

Pastor Moore stood in front of the altar. One had come. Only one? He swallowed and closed his eyes. He wanted revival, and God sent him a teenage boy. He shook his head and took a deep breath. No, this was not time for doubt. Hadn't he prayed for at least one? He sighed.

God, help that boy who came today. Manifest Yourself in him. And help me to stop doubting the small things in life.

Peace settled over Pastor Moore. He opened his eyes and walked down the aisle. One was enough.

†

Daniel stepped out into the warm day. Colorful leaves crunched underneath his feet as he walked down the church steps. People gathered around the church to fellowship under the cloudy sky. Daniel wove his way through the crowd to where Art, Sean, and Matthew stood with a group of teenagers under a skeletal tree. What were the odds that they would attend the same church? Art held up the morning bulletin as he approached.

"What do you think, Daniel? Will you be able to come to the Labor Day Retreat?"

Daniel scratched his chin. He looked over at his aunt and uncle who were talking with a young woman and two toddlers. "I hope so."

Art winked. "It'll be great. Charleston, South Carolina, is awesome at the end of summer, especially on the lake. You still have a few weeks. Think about it."

Daniel stuffed his hands in the pockets of his slacks. "I will."

A group of girls passed by him, giggling and whispering to one another. From the corner of his eye, Daniel noticed one girl from the youth group standing at the bottom of the church steps alone. There was something familiar about her. He turned. Could it be? The girl raised her head from searching in her purse and Daniel grinned. He walked toward her.

"Neala?"

Neala looked in Daniel's direction, eyes wide. "Daniel?" she laughed nervously as he came closer and glanced around. "I...I didn't know you came to Trinity."

He winked. "It's my first day again. I might need another tour."

She laughed. "Any other day I would give you one, but I'm actually supposed to meet Reganne in a few minutes."

He nodded slowly, noting how her eyes darted back and forth to a place beyond them. He held out his hand to her. "Well, it was nice seeing you."

She hesitated. Then, she bit her lower lip and took his outstretched hand. "Yeah, you too."

"See you Monday?"

Neala turned but nodded slightly. "Sure, Monday."

Daniel watched her as she quickly crossed the parking lot. She slipped her Bible into her shoulder bag as she approached a blue sedan pulling into the parking lot. The graffiti-trimmed car was packed to the brim with Neala's friends from school. She squeezed inside next to Elliot.

Their laughter echoed across the parking lot, a sound Daniel hadn't heard since the first day of school when some of the class partook in morning prayer. Daniel sighed. Well, he couldn't be friends with all three hundred students at Chancellor, but he could be friends to them.

They drove by the front entrance of the church, honking the horn loudly as they passed. Daniel waved at the group as they crossed the intersection.

While his hand was still raised, he heard a mother walk by with two of her young children.

She shook her head and pointed at the sedan. "Those are the kind of people you do not talk to, not ever, about anything. Half of them will probably end up in jail by the end of the year." As she spoke to her son, she tugged on her children's hands. "They shouldn't even be allowed on the church property."

Daniel watched them stare after the blue sedan with wide eyes. Daniel frowned. What if someday God wanted that boy to talk to those kinds of people about Him? He shook his head and walked back toward the other teenage boys. They were not people; they were souls.

God, help those children to see the truth.

He looked up at the church entrance as his uncle shook hands with Pastor Moore. The man looked weary after his morning sermon. But it had been worth it. He still didn't know why he'd gone to the altar today. He had not known what to pray about, but had felt the Spirit telling him to go. So, he had gone, waited, and then returned to his seat. Perhaps it was his orphan's heart that cried out for the comfort and peace of the altar. Perhaps it was something more. Only God knew.

"Daniel!"

Daniel turned toward the sound of his aunt's voice. She motioned for him to come to the car. He looked back at Art, Sean, and Matthew. With a shrug, he waved at them and hurried toward his guardian's gold Camry. Uncle Devon followed close behind. Once they were all in the car, Daniel sent a silent prayer for safety as his uncle maneuvered out of the crowded parking lot.

While they waited to turn at the intersection, Daniel glanced out the window to the street in front of them. His exploring eyes paused. His breath caught in his throat. Chancellor?

For the first time, he noticed the big brick building he attended was right across the street from his church. Daniel glanced behind him. He smiled. The entrances of the two buildings were parallel. He noticed Mr. Pierce crossing the walkway that separated the two establishments. No wonder so many Chancellor students had appeared amongst the sea of faces today.

Daniel settled back in his seat. He couldn't help but wonder if his mother was smiling with him at the structure God was creating around him in this new location. It would be her secret smile, the one that said God was all the sanctuary in the world that Daniel needed. Daniel's throat closed at the thought of his mother's smile. His turbulent heart didn't hurt as much as it had this morning but the pain was still there. He swallowed hard. The altar had helped. Healing would come.

"So Daniel, you like soccer?"

Uncle Devon's voice brought Daniel back to the present. He glanced at his uncle in the rearview mirror. He shook his head.

"No sir, I love soccer."

He chuckled. "I see. Well, while Aunt Lisa gets lunch ready, we can kick the ball around in the backyard. Does that sound good?"

Daniel nodded. The very thought of playing with the soccer ball again made his heart pump. It was about time he tested his last gift from his Michigan league. The brand new soccer ball with signatures from his former teammates lay untouched under his bed.

"Oh, talking about soccer, Mr. Pierce said that they are short a player at Chancellor High. The tryouts were last spring but maybe they could let you try to get in. Art, Sean, Matthew and a few other boys are part of the team. It is one of the best soccer programs in the area."

Daniel almost laughed. Could this day get any better? "I'll call Art tonight and see what he says. That would be awesome."

Uncle Devon smiled. Aunt Lisa reached over and squeezed his hand. Daniel swallowed hard. They were doing the best they could to make this Daniel's home, and he couldn't complain about this added bonus. He smiled. The struggles he met on the soccer field were synonymous with life. To reach life's goals, there were many obstacles to step around. And, no matter how many times one was pushed back, failure was out of the question. This was why Daniel's mother and he had been such soccer fanatics. That was why he still was. Now God presented this new opportunity to pursue his soccer passion. God was continuously surprising him at Chancellor High. What would He do next?

CHAPTER 7
ORDER

Roy stood resolute at the head of the board table. He placed his hands against the polished wooden surface and looked each individual in the eye. "This school can only progress in one way. We need to stop being held back by these unnecessary programs."

A severe-looking woman to his right cleared her throat. "And where do you propose to put those funds if the programs are cut out?"

Roy grinned. "The best place to invest is the sports program."

He reached for the folder in front of him and produced a stack of papers. He passed the charts of speculation around the room. The board members perused his plan as he illustrated each point. He knew the moment they accepted it. He could see it through the light in their eyes. He took a deep breath. It was time to close the deal.

"The future of this school lies in the soccer program. Bring in the best players and invest more in the program. Give them scholarships. Give them more opportunities. Get rid of this backwater mindset and cut out what is wrong with the school. Cut out what shouldn't be there. Give the students a true sense of our motto."

The head of the board laid the papers on the desk. "What do you propose we do about our principal?"

Roy shrugged. "The purpose of the school will be set by the leadership."

"We can't cut him out completely."

"Well, that is your decision…but how many students will change their purpose if he stays? How far do you want to go with this incentive?"

There was a moment of silence. The decision lay over the board like a thick blanket. Whatever decision they made would change everything.

The director stood to his feet. "If you ask me, I want to go all the way with the proposed changes."

He nodded once at Roy and then turned to the rest of the attendees. "Let's put it to a vote."

Roy exited the room to leave them to the vote. For a few minutes, he paced back and forth, his footfalls muffled by the plush carpet underneath him. They actually listened to him. They heard what he had to say. It was time for his changes to take place. He stopped pacing and leaned against the white wall. *Is this really happening?*

Standing here alone, with the prospect of success right under his nose, was nerve-racking. If he got the position, it would mean the world. Some might call it lowly, but it was a position of power. He clenched his fists. Slowly, he could take back what was taken from him years ago. Justice was at hand.

The door opened. The first person to step out was the director. His eyes revealed all Roy needed to know. His heart leapt to his throat. The position was his. Chancellor High would never be the same again.

CHAPTER 8
ROOKIE

Mrs. Morales stood up behind her desk. On cue, composition notebooks slammed shut and students capped their pens. Daniel glanced at the wall clock above the classroom door. Five more minutes and another day would be over. As he collected his books from the tray beneath his desk, he saw Mrs. Morales hold up her hand. The room stilled, an effect only she could accomplish with such a gesture. She cleared her throat.

"Due to the assembly tomorrow, we will not have this class. I know most of you are pleased with this. However, you will not escape without a considerable amount of work to keep your minds sharp. During your Labor Day Weekend, I want each of you to begin researching for your term paper."

Daniel's heart mirrored the collective groan that swept across the English classroom. His shoulders slumped. So much for his having three free days. Mrs. Morales waited for the room to quiet before continuing.

"The subject this year is: Politics in your Comfort Zone. I really want to see depth of thought and passion in every thesis. Feel free to focus on any law or politician that catches your interest. You are seniors. I expect to see you raise the standards from the past. Negativity is allowed but no vulgarity."

The dismissal bell rang. Students jumped from their seats, eager to escape the classroom and exchange it for a free afternoon. Mrs. Morales wisely withheld the rest of her speech. She nodded, letting her students go, while she called out above the tromping of a dozen feet in a final attempt to be heard.

"Surprise me!"

Daniel nodded, although she would not see him amongst the other heads around her. He slipped into the hallway, heading down the stairs toward his locker. He would surprise himself if he turned in a paper only half full of grammar mistakes. Ah, the requirements of English class. Who had convinced him to take the Advanced Placement Grammar and Composition? Daniel shook his head. Sometimes having a sharp mind could be such a burden. Opening his locker, he slid literature and grammar books into their respective places on the shelf. They settled, happy to be out of his unenthusiastic hands. At least another Thursday was over.

As he swung his backpack over his shoulder, Daniel's eyes fell on the gym bag sitting at the bottom of his locker. It was settled quite uncomfortably, looking up at its owner as if to remind him of what lay ahead. Daniel's stomach tightened. His day wasn't quite over yet.

Both of his guardians had insisted he take a chance at this soccer position. Although Daniel hadn't needed much prodding, his nerves were begging him to reconsider. Daniel shook himself. He grabbed his gym bag and placed it on his opposite shoulder. This was not an exam; it was a tryout. His hands still trembled and adrenaline pumped through his veins as he moved away from his locker toward the front doors of Chancellor High.

Art, Matthew, and Sean met Daniel at the entrance of the locker room. His friends had teased him endlessly all day, making it nearly impossible for him to feel confident. Even now, as he walked toward them, they bent their heads together in a whisper. It was a conspiracy! He grinned and rolled his eyes.

"Hey, Man!" Matthew called out.

"Hey."

He had to stretch a bit to reach his giant fists. He turned to meet the fists of Sean and Art with one of his own. Then Art slapped him on the back.

"Are you ready to get this done?"

He winked, "Let's go play some fútbol."

They all laughed. Then, their bodies energized by the upcoming practice, they led Daniel toward the locker room. Daniel slipped into his gear. It felt good to slide the equipment over his skin again.

Once all of them were ready, Art pulled Daniel beside him. "Let me make the introductions to Coach. He usually trusts me."

"Always," corrected Sean.

Daniel smiled.

Art shrugged off the comment. "Come on," he prodded, "we're late."

In a swift movement, Art opened the side door of the locker room, and Daniel stepped onto Chancellor's soccer field. Part of Daniel felt himself still moving, following Art toward a group of men on the side of the field; but his eyes and heart froze. He stared at the field as if he'd found lost treasure.

Players milled about the emerald turf, dressed in jerseys of different colors. Pristine white lines marked the boundaries of the field while at the same time embracing those within them. And the goals, like two guardians, stood erect over the scene, their nets spread wide while their posts were deeply rooted underground. They stood in anticipation for what was to come.

The stands were empty, but in Daniel's mind, he could imagine the metal bleachers filled to capacity. He could hear the noise of the crowd and feel the electricity of that first game. He breathed deeply. Ah, here was a place of dreams. He knew then, standing on that field, that he had come here for more than the thrill of the game. Here, he was so close to grasping his game of life. Someday he would be able to run in wider fields, score in larger stadiums. Perhaps that day, he would hold his aspirations in his hands. Perhaps.

"Excuse me, Coach."

Art's voice shocked Daniel into reality. He zeroed in on the group of men his friend had stopped in front of. He straightened. He would work for that someday, but he had to qualify here first.

The coach turned toward his player. He towered above Daniel, his muscles bulging through his coach's polo. His face was lined with years, but the long, steady strides he used to reach them indicated he was a man who defied age.

He addressed Art. "Yes, what is it?"

Art motioned toward Daniel. "My friend would like to try out for the empty spot on the team."

Daniel stepped forward as the coach turned toward him. "My name's Daniel Stevens."

The coach took Daniel's hand in a firm, knuckle splitting grip. Daniel stepped back, flexing his fingers.

After the handshake, the coach looked away from him. He flipped a few pages on the clipboard he was holding. Daniel glanced at Art. His friend kept his eyes on the man before him, so Daniel followed his lead. For a moment, the only sound between them was the scratching of a pen as the coach wrote on the clipboard's sheets. Finally, Coach Wilkins looked back at Daniel.

"You're late on your first day. Do you have any idea how big soccer is in Chancellor High?"

He cleared his throat. "No, Sir, I just moved..."

"It's huge, boy! We have gone to State for three consecutive years. We play clean but rough. We don't take the building of this team lightly." He sighed, shaking his head. "And yet you come, hoping for a spot. I guess you think you're good enough?"

He shifted his weight from one foot to another. "Well, I..."

"What do you know about soccer, Daniel?"

"Everything. Its origin, modern techniques, rise in popularity for the United States. I..."

"Have you played anywhere besides your backyard or family reunion?"

"Yes, Sir. My church in Michigan had a league. I was the captain."

Coach lowered his clipboard. "Well, we already have a captain, but I've lost one of my top defenders. His shoes are impossible to fill. I'm not promising you anything, Rookie, but feel free to join us."

He looked beyond Daniel to where Sean and Matthew hovered a few yards away. The coach raised his voice. "The rookie and Sean will be on the red team. Art and Matt are blue today. Grab your jerseys and get ready for drills."

Art nodded. "Right, Coach."

Daniel followed Art to a heap of bags near the dugout. He reached into one while Sean instructed Daniel to grab a jersey from the other. Inside, he untangled red jerseys, finding one that fit him. He slipped it over his tee. Art winked at him.

"Good luck," he said.

Then, Art and Matthew ran toward the right side of the field. Daniel followed Sean to the left side of the field, eyeing the other students that had exchanged their daily clothes for red jerseys. He nodded at them in passing. Some nodded in return, but most rolled their eyes and continued stretching. He exhaled. He turned toward Sean and asked for each name in turn. He used small details, a scar on one teammate, a tattoo on the other, to identify each. He would need that, and their names, during the game. Hopefully, they would learn his soon.

Daniel stretched his calves and thighs. He loosened his shoulders, rolling them away from the collarbone. Amidst his stretches, he paused and glanced across the field. On the other end, the eyes of the opposing team looked his way. Wherever he glanced, he could see different pairs of eyes zeroed in on him. There were critical eyes from the coaches, mistrusting eyes from the team members, and hopeful eyes from his friends. The soccer field suddenly lost its glow and was replaced by a stadium of criticism.

How could he please so many people? How could he bring value to himself in the eyes of superiors? Should he play clean or mean? Daniel took a deep breath and closed his eyes.

Father.

The noise died away. The pressure of what would soon be faded. Daniel's breath fell into a restful pattern. Then he met another pair of eyes, etched within his soul. These eyes were shadowed by the unknown and yet glowed with the light of life. They were not full of pressure or arrogance but pride, love, and assurance. As long as he focused on these eyes, all would be well.

The sharp trill of the coach's whistle soared through the field. Daniel opened his eyes and drew back to the present. He smiled. The field of dreams was glowing again, daring the rookie to take a shot. He nodded. He took his place behind Sean, ready to run the first drill. As his turn drew nearer, he glanced at the sky. *From whence cometh my help.*

He took a deep breath. He knew this sport. He knew how to pull himself from within and let it all out. He knew how to run and pass, score and strategize. He only had to please One and play a game clean enough to prove His power. Daniel ran forward.

In this, too, he would please Him.

†

Roy watched the boy he'd called rookie run down the field. This was where they all failed. Here, in an apparent moment of glory, the boy would show his ego. He picked up his pen, drew the clipboard close. No one could replace Santos. He grimaced and waited.

Two members of the red team spread out before Daniel. Sean was in perfect position to score, but anyone who was in Daniel's position might think the same of himself. It was time to strategize or strike. The blue team relaxed instinctively. They knew what was coming; every other tryout was the same. Roy clicked his pen.

In a flash of black and white, the ball slid to Sean. The moment the rookie passed his victory to his teammate, Roy lost his breath. It was beautiful. The ball slid into the goal, taking the blue goalie by surprise. For the first time since Santos' departure, the red team won their mock game. The players went wild. Even the blue team caught on to the celebration as they headed toward the locker room.

Roy smirked as the throng of teenagers zoomed past him. He dipped his head when Daniel tried to catch his eyes. He scribbled on the chart in his hands. Sometimes this job was worth its lousy pay.

After finishing his notes, Roy headed toward his assistant coach. He patted the short parent rep and referee on the shoulder.

"Hey, Mackenzie," Roy handed him the clipboard, "the boy's in."

Mackenzie looked at the chart. A knowing grin parted his lips. "I was going to put him on anyway. He's got amazing footwork. Did you see how quickly he caught on to his teammates names? And then of course there was the last play. That kid's got the stuff. He's real gifted."

Roy nodded. "That he is."

He glanced at the field before him. He sighed. It wasn't a bad way to end the day. He deserved to see one more display of talent before he let this go. Coach Wilkins looked back at Mackenzie. "Hey, when the kid takes you guys to nationals remember it was my call." He added silently, "My last call."

Mackenzie's smile faded. "Are you sure you know what you're doing? Paperwork doesn't become you."

Roy frowned. That was certain, but there were too many educational gaps all around him. Yes, he was doing the right thing. When all of this was over, others would see. He winked at his assistant.

"I'll be fine." He motioned toward the locker room. "Go give the rookie the news, and take care of him. He's all yours now."

Mackenzie extended his hand. "It's been nice working with you."

He parted with his assistant. Then, he headed down the tunnel toward the school parking lot, and away from what had once been his dream job. He paused near his Mustang and looked back at the enormous field behind the school building. He had dreamed there once. He had been a boy with hopes and a real gift, just like that rookie. But life had gotten under his skin. Hypocrisy had rent him apart and disappointments formed him into a hard man who labored with others to make what would never be his, theirs. The time for such menial tasks was at an end.

Roy climbed into his car and turned the key to rev up the engine. There was no turning back. He put the car into reverse. It was time to walk away from something good, and embrace something better.

CHAPTER 9
CHOSEN

"Go through another G scale and pick up the speed."

Neala sat straighter on the piano bench and ran her fingers over the ivory keys. It was a wonder that Chancellor's new band director even allowed a piano amongst her array of equipment.

Ms. Marble was more interested in drums, keyboards, and electric guitars than clarinets, saxophones, and classical piano. She knew about them, taught about them, even tuned them, but her sensibilities ran more toward a rock band than an orchestra.

Neala finished the G scale and ran through it again. The spring concert was going to be interesting. Her ears still rang with the cacophony Ms. Marble had directed in band today. It was fun for others. Band had become less precise, geared toward the modern fad of "metal expression." But it only made her fall behind in her goals.

She didn't care for the sound of drums or vibrations of the electric guitar. How could band be a solace if she couldn't lose herself in classical renditions from the greats? Of course, she wouldn't complain. Who would believe Reganne's best buddy enjoyed stuffy classics over hard rock? It didn't fit her school profile.

But here, there was a feeling of sophistication. With only her music filling the room, she could capture a pedigree of calm that once had been her band class. Resisting the urge to follow her fingers and disrupt the normal cadence of the lesson, Neala lifted her fingers and glanced at Ms. Marble, waiting.

If Mrs. Maldonado were still here, she would be learning different tricks and techniques. She even may have moved on to the organ that sat in her teacher's house. But, her teacher's love for something greater than music had carried her away. And yet, her teacher's confidence in her had been established by their last memory together. She still remembered the summer wedding. She remembered her teacher's insistence that Neala be the pianist.

When she closed her eyes, she could smell the lilies that surrounded the piano at which she'd sat, could hear the violin accompanist, and could feel her fingers run through the wedding march, and later, through the song "From This Moment On." She'd known then that she was losing the most humble maestra of true, classical music that ever lived. It was a moment she would never forget. Nor did she want to because all that was left now was this piano and a teacher that did not carry as much passion as the former.

Ms. Marble came toward Neala, her bubble skirt swaying as she walked. Neala sighed. She wanted to move forward, but Ms. Marble insisted she play the electric keyboard before moving on to the organ. She cringed at the thought. Still, she pressed on. She was determined to wait, for this, and only this. Ms. Marble stopped beside her.

"Very good, Hon. I think we'll forego the keyboard today. I need to step out. Start your C scales. I'll be right back."

Neala positioned her fingers over the keys but gritted her teeth. She knew her scales to perfection. She began her second round, eyes on Ms. Marble as she exited the band room. The young teacher pulled a phone from her skirt pocket and scurried down the hall toward the staff break room. The door closed silently behind her. Neala glanced at the wall clock. Ten minutes, and her private lesson would be over. She grinned. Ms. Marble wasn't coming back.

She played the scale for the exact sixty seconds it would take her teacher to reach the break room. Then, she slowly lifted her fingers, letting the warm up exercises fade. She exhaled. Tension released its grip on her shoulders. Finally, she was alone.

Her eyes opened, returning to the keys before her. They ran over each ivory key in turn. Now, without the pressure to rein in their musical tendencies, they came to life. Each one vied for the attention of her hand. She smiled a smile carrying a secret meant only for her and the piano keys. She positioned her hands, each finger poised. She really must show them true care, for their sakes, and hers. But, what should she play?

Neala closed her eyes. Behind her eyelids, musical notes formed and lined up. She knew better than to orchestrate them. Music lent itself to her and she merely claimed it. Her soul was the director, her fingers the administrators, and her ears the sharpest critics. Ever since her fingers had touched the keyboard when she was five, she'd known these moments would come. And when they did, she allowed them to consume her. Here, safely settled on the piano bench, she could scale the highest mountains and deepest valleys of her dreams.

When the notes finally settled, she followed the composition flowing through her mind. She recognized the first strains immediately: "Danny Boy." She smiled. How appropriate. She'd been avoiding Daniel and the hurt she'd caused when she mentioned this song. But it was for his sake, not her own. Her fingers slipped, and she paused. Ok. Maybe it's for my sake too. The truth was simple. He seemed like a person who could offer her more than she could hope to repay. She knew better than to become a debtor to anyone, especially a guy. In the end, he was human. He would disappoint her like everyone else.

Neala's eyebrows rose in surprise as the notes of "Danny Boy" faded into a different song. She followed through, her ears filling with the tune of "Amazing Grace." She frowned. How odd, she had played this only once at church. She had promised herself to forget it. But here it was, beckoning her to relive its glory. Neala complied, for now. Maybe it was her internal clock's way of reminding her that tonight was youth night.

Something new began to play beneath Neala's fingers. Both songs lured one another into a synonymous tune. Their notes overlapped with precision, dancing in rhythm to Neala's beating heart. She began to tremble. She could stop anytime, but her heart didn't dare and her hands refused. And then she knew. She must play this compilation; she must answer its call, for it was a fountain of emotions that jumped from the secret parts of her soul.

So, Neala continued. Her fingers traced both songs, melding them into one. In its place, a new song emerged, claiming her, whispering its secrets into her ear. It filled her with a hunger so alarming that her heart clamored for more. She let the secrets of the song wash over her.

Amidst the notes, there was love lost and love gained, mercy absent and mercy found, hope on the edge of a dark precipice and hope renewed by the promise of eternity. The music lent both pain and healing unlike anything she'd ever experienced. She grasped for the healing. She held it tightly, even when tears marred her cheeks and her hands throbbed with exhaustion. She clung to it until the last strain faded from her mind and her fingers released the last keys. Only then did the trance end, the hope began to fade, and the song's echo beckoned her to open her eyes.

She breathed deeply. Her hands fell into her lap. She stared at them. She had never been presented with such a tangible tune nor had she lost it so quickly.

"Bravo!"

Neala's head shot up. Ms. Marble stood at the entrance of the band room, a toothy smile on her face. Neala wiped tears from her eyes and straightened. Her head pounded.

"You heard that?" she asked.

Ms. Marble shrugged, "I got the end of it."

Relief washed over her as her teacher approached. The song was still hers alone. She glanced up at Ms. Marble as she stopped beside her.

Ms. Marble furrowed her brow. "Did you use sheet music?"

She shook her head. "No, just my head. I guess my brain is my music sheet."

"Incredible! Well, tell you what, I'm going to give you a solo on the keyboard for the spring concert. We'll leave this piano behind and see what you can do with contemporary pieces, starting tomorrow. Good enough?"

Neala bit her lower lip. She looked down at the familiar piano keys. Dare she leave them behind and conform to Ms. Marble's modern musical theory? She sighed. At least modern theory provided safety. She wouldn't dare bare her soul across the mechanical keyboard. If she ever played her song at a public concert…Neala's heart dropped to her stomach. *That can never happen.*

She turned back to Ms. Marble. "Sounds good to me."

Ms. Marble winked. "That a girl. Come on, your mom is waiting outside, and I have a date to get ready for." Ms. Marble's eyes twinkled as she turned toward the exit again, expecting Neala to follow. With one more glance toward the piano, Neala rose to follow.

She propped the door open with her foot and turned to switch the light off in the band room. As she did, she spotted a shadow on the opposite side of the curtain that separated band from choir. She paused, narrowed her eyes. Was there someone in here?

She blinked and the shadow disappeared. *Just my imagination.* Shaking her head, she turned and followed Ms. Marble down the hallway and to the stairs.

Perhaps it had been an angel, coming down to peruse her musical abilities. Neala sighed. *Angels.* Maybe one did exist just for her. It could keep the secrets of her soul in its pocket. It could have her song, and only the two of them would know her hungers.

†

"Daniel? Do you know what this email is all about?"

Daniel looked up from his Advanced Calculus book. Aunt Lisa stood in the entrance of the dining room, a piece of paper in her hands.

"What email?" he asked.

Aunt Lisa chewed on her lower lip. "It's from the school office. It says that the parents have been asked to attend the assembly this Friday. 'The administration will be discussing changes in the school's infrastructure effective after Labor Day Weekend.' Did they mention anything to you guys?"

He shook his head. "It's probably no big deal."

"Well, I'm not sure we're going to be able to make it."

He looked up at Aunt Lisa and grinned. "So I'll tell you what happened at dinnertime."

Her eyes widened. "Dinner? Oh, my lasagna!"

Daniel chuckled and gathered his homework into a neat pile. He heard the oven door squeak open and his aunt's hurried footsteps as she tried to save the night's dinner. He looked at his watch. Perfect. He would have time to make the surprise for The Crusaders and maybe run around with the soccer ball to get rid of Calculus tension. This class was ungodly!

He winced as glass shattered in the kitchen. Soccer first. There was no way he was stepping near the kitchen computer while Aunt Lisa was cooking.

As he passed the kitchen on his way to his room, his aunt called out to him.

"Daniel! You have an email from the soccer coach. I left it on your bed."

Daniel paused. He took a deep breath before continuing to his room. Here went nothing. It was time to see if he had played well enough on Chancellor's field. He stopped in front of the door.

Thy will be done, Lord.

Daniel pushed the door open. He laid his books on his computer desk and then approached the bed. Tentatively, he picked up the piece of paper.

Daniel,
This is just to inform you that you will be expected at practice tomorrow, immediately after school. Bring soccer shorts and cleats.   -Coach Mackenzie

Daniel exhaled. He made the cut. With a shout, he reached under the bed and grabbed his soccer ball. Who said nerds couldn't like sports? Whistling the tune of "Amazing Grace," he headed to the back yard.

CHAPTER 10
ASSEMBLY

Daniel stuffed the posters into his gym bag. All around him, students rushed up the stairs toward the gym. They chatted amongst themselves, discussing plans for the upcoming three-day weekend. Daniel thrust his gym bag into his locker. He slid out a single copy of the poster and rolled it up. He had big plans for this weekend too.

Once he locked up his belongings, Daniel joined the milling crowd. Bodies pressed against him. Shouts rang in his ears. Giggles and a few curse words pounded through his mind. Daniel wound his way through both strangers and classmates. Everyone ignored the reprimands from their teachers to slow down and keep quiet. Who cared about following instructions? It was time for the assembly!

The gym's interior was more subdued. Daniel took a moment to breathe. A few whispers and giggles overshadowed the usual celebratory mood. Today, new presences filled the gym. Seated in rows of wooden chairs, parents sat impatiently awaiting the declaration about school-wide changes. Daniel turned toward the bleachers.

He spotted Art near the top of the bleachers. Sean and Matthew waved down at him from Art's side. They motioned for Daniel to join them. Art removed his sweater from a spot at his left side. Daniel grinned. He could always count on them to save him a seat. He made his way over and between the students already seated to reach the high perch his friends had chosen.

When he finally got to his reserved seat next to Art, he exhaled and smiled. He let his eyes wander a bit, ignoring the gaze of all three of his friends. They questioned him with their eyes. Daniel chuckled, turned toward them, and held out the poster. They greedily took his response into their hands. Daniel surrendered the paper. This was something he figured God would forgive them for being greedy about.

They opened the rolled up paper to reveal the artwork within. An image of the Holy Grail stood in the middle of the page with a Bible filling up its recesses. A sea of faces filled the background, creating the illusion that the grail was floating amongst all ethnicities of the earth. The only thing left to do was to pick up the grail and examine its contents. The top of the page read: The Crusaders: Join us in discovering eternal treasure. The bottom of the page listed all the information about the Bible study.

Daniel let them look over the poster and then leaned in to get their opinions. Art laughed and slapped Daniel on the back. Matthew whistled, shaking his head. Sean just continued to stare. His wide eyes absorbed each detail. This was a high compliment for someone who despised any form of art. Daniel couldn't help but feel a sense of pride rise in his chest. The rings under his eyes and exhaustion in his bones were nothing compared to the doors this was going to open and all the souls that might be saved. The Crusaders had big plans for this weekend. They were going to fill up their Bible study room, even if they had to offer breakfast every morning. From posters in the school hallways to blogs and Facebook, The Crusaders were ready to expand. It was unfair to keep their sanctuary a secret any longer.

As they waited for the assembly to begin, Daniel explained to them the layout of the tract he designed to go with the poster. By the time the world history teacher stood to call the assembly to order, they all had decided to meet at Art's house after practice and set up The Crusaders blog. Mr. Peterson cut off their planning when he stood on the gym stage and spoke into the microphone.

Daniel shook with excitement when the usual school spirit shout ensued. He let loose his spirit with more energy than ever before. Even Sean stood to shout out above the crowd. Daniel felt no need to contain his laughter. They had a reason to shout that was buried deep in their souls. This was the life worth living. For the first time in months, the foreignness was melting away. No doubt about it, he belonged in Chancellor High.

After a while, the students were asked to sit. There would be no competitions today, not with the gym full of parents. Daniel looked for Mr. Pierce in the line of Chancellor's faculty on the stage. What crazy stunt would he pull today?

Daniel spotted Mr. Pierce in the center of the teacher panel. The robust man looked grim today. He wasn't joking with his staff nor dressed in his usual eccentric uniform to initiate cheers from the student body. Daniel glanced at Art. If he had noticed how subdued the principal was, it didn't seem to bother him. He whispered with Matthew, his anxiety level near zero. Daniel relaxed. Mr. Pierce probably wanted to keep a formal atmosphere. He chuckled at the thought of Mr. Pierce clowning around in front of the parents.

When everyone was settled, Mr. Pierce stood and took the microphone. He looked down at the parents. For a moment, he said nothing, just stared down, gathering his thoughts. Then, his booming voice filled the gym.

"I'm honored by the number of parents finding time to attend today. I am always pleased to see concern for the well-being of your children. I know you received the email, so I will not waste my time in telling you why this meeting was called. Big things are taking place today." Mr. Pierce's voice softened. "Things out of my control."

He lifted his attention from the parents to the three hundred students filling the bleachers behind them. His gaze moved across the student body. For a moment, Daniel was sure he was gazing right at him. Daniel held his breath. *Something's wrong.*

Mr. Pierce looked back at the parents and continued. "A week ago, the academy director confronted me with a few errors he had noticed within our school's core. He asked me to change them. I refused." A ripple of unease spread across the room. Mr. Pierce smiled sadly. "Hopefully, someday, all of you will understand my reasons. I love this school and have great hopes for the students. Sometimes, though, life presents us with difficult choices. Today, I'm resigning my position as principal of Chancellor High School."

No one spoke, but heads turned and eyes widened. Daniel felt regret shoot through him. Mr. Pierce had set spiritual foundations for this school's campus. He was the initiator and first member of The Crusaders. It would be sad to see him go. He silently prayed that he would get a better job soon. He silently prayed that he would find a way to thank him for the path he'd left behind.

After a few minutes of silence, Mr. Pierce inhaled deeply. His chin trembled as he resumed speaking. "I know this is sudden, but it is necessary. No matter what changes, or who comes to take my place, know that my thoughts and prayers for each of you will remain unchanged. I hope you will all find ways to influence a small corner of this world, and always, take a stand for what's right. In the end, that's all that matters." Mr. Pierce let his words sink in for a moment. Then, he sighed. "Now, without further adieu, I will pass this microphone to your new principal. He is no stranger. All of you know him well. Please welcome Coach Wilkins, the newly chosen administrator of Chancellor High School."

As Coach Wilkins rose from his seat to take the microphone from Mr. Pierce, the shock reverberated twofold across the room. No one moved, even when the men shook hands. Suddenly, someone above Daniel started clapping. Awakened by the sound, the rest of the room followed suit.

Daniel glanced at Art. Not once during practice or the big announcement about Daniel's position on the team had there been mention of Coach Wilkins leaving the team. He must have known. Decisions like these weren't made overnight. What happened to his boast about soccer being top priority? Why would he risk the season? Daniel zeroed in on the new speaker. Chills crawled up his spine. Coach Wilkins was the last one he would've expected to be principal.

Coach Wilkins held up his hands to silence the crowd. He struggled between keeping a straight face and breaking out into a full-fledged grin. The battle ended with a small smirk capturing the corners of his mouth. When the crowd quieted, he cleared his throat.

"Mr. Pierce, you have been with us for years. In fact, I remember you teaching my geometry class when I was a freshman." Laughter rippled across the room. "We're going to miss you terribly. Your shoes are too big and my feet are too small. But I promise you I will do my best. Like you said, life is full of choices." Coach Wilkins turned toward the parents and students. "And choices often bring change. My promise extends to those of you sitting in this room today. I will try to exceed your highest expectations. It won't be easy..."

Daniel leaned back, happy that no one occupied the bleacher behind him. All around him, others shifted into more comfortable positions. This was going to be a long speech.

For twenty minutes, Coach Wilkins droned on about his new policy. He was determined to make this transition as easy as possible. It was an odd transition. Calling him coach one day and principal the next would require some practice. Daniel had a feeling Coach already had today's strategy planned out.

As if to confirm Daniel's thoughts, Coach told his players that Mackenzie was now the head of the Conqueror soccer team. All in all, Daniel saw no need for his guardians to have attended today. Their absence wasn't too much of a loss. Mr. Pierce would be missed, but his retirement was forthcoming. Daniel closed his eyes, waiting for the dismissal bell to ring. He was craving that soccer practice.

"Before I dismiss, there is one more change I'd like to address. We are a charter school, but government funded nonetheless. There are amendments we have been neglecting. The director saw the problem, and I readily agreed. Mr. Pierce didn't, which is why today finds me in this new position. Within these walls, there isn't enough separation between church and state."

Daniel furrowed his brow as he opened his eyes. He glanced at Mr. Pierce. Why had he challenged the students to take a stand instead of remember him? Could it be?

"From this point on," continued Coach Wilkins, "there will be no religious activity on campus. This includes the prayers at the opening and closing of each class. Of course, in the lunchroom, the students may feel free to say grace. I wouldn't want to cause indigestion."

71

A few of the guys in the bleachers above Daniel laughed outright. Daniel frowned as he continued.

"Furthermore, The Crusaders Bible study is null and void. Being that only four students attend, I view the whole thing an erroneous financial investment. Additionally, I believe it to be unconstitutional. Room 400 will now be used as a tutoring center."

Daniel straightened; his spine stiffened. No! Each word that Coach Wilkins spoke stung his mind like icy, cold water. No prayer... The Crusaders...null and void. Daniel clutched the rim of the bleachers until his knuckles turned colorless. Every bone in his body tensed. He saw a few students hand out high fives. He couldn't tell the reaction of the parents. From his viewpoint, they sat motionless, unwilling to change what was now in motion.

Daniel turned to his friends. Art's jaw was now a tightly wound spring waiting on the edge of explosion. Matthew covered his eyes with two meaty fists. Every bone in the giant's body was taut as if he were preparing for battle, but he forced himself to hold back, choosing to turn to his Creator for vengeance. Then there was Sean. His face was as unreadable as always and his eyes looked straight ahead. In his hand, he clutched the poster as if he were clinging to the last ember of their dying fire.

Daniel turned forward again. Coach Wilkins was talking. "Chancellor is about high education, not High Powers. We are here to fashion your children's brains, not their souls. Trust me, things are going to improve without religion playing on their minds."

"Amen!" cried out one of the parents. Full-fledged laughter and nervous chuckles mingled throughout the room.

Every nerve in Daniel's body screamed for him to swipe that smile off of Wilkins's face. They were not mocking religion; they were mocking God! And he allowed it. Daniel put pressure on his feet, felt strength rise to his calves. Someone had to end this.

A grip on his forearm stopped Daniel's intentions and actions. As Coach Wilkins wrapped up the assembly, Daniel looked into Art's eyes. A desire parallel to Daniel's burned in the Crusader's eyes but was accompanied by a grave warning. Art flicked his eyes upward.

Daniel exhaled. Someone would stop this; but not him, not today. He conceded to the fact, but rage and fear still ran through his body. With just a few words, Coach Wilkins had destroyed Daniel's sanctuary at Chancellor.

A few minutes later, the dismissal bell rang. The gym's inhabitants stood and rushed out to greet one of the last days of Indian summer. All except four young boys. Stoic and shocked, they sat on the bleachers, waiting for the tide of humanity to pass. Soccer practice didn't even cross their minds. Their world was falling apart, and they had no idea how to comfort each other.

Coach Wilkins passed them, his voice ironically light, his eyes never once passing in their direction. Why shouldn't he be carefree? He had decreed his worst for what he thought was best. Why should he care about four disappointed teenage boys?

Daniel was the first to speak after Wilkins exited. "He can't do this," he whispered.

Sean laughed. It was a dry and resigned laugh that cut through all of them. He crumpled the poster in his hand. "He just did."

With a mighty heave, Sean threw the poster across the gym. Then, he marched down the bleachers. Matthew, Art, and Daniel followed suit. As they exited, their plans sailed through the humid gym and landed in a crumpled mass at the base of the microphone stand.

†

Neala had to wake up. She waited for the alarm clock to shake her out of this nightmare. That face and voice that threatened to take over Chancellor was the visage of fear that visited her every day. He was the predominant wedge between mother and daughter. Surely this was a dream. Her mother had never hinted at the possibility. Was the deceit purposeful? How dare he change so much of Chancellor's foundation? *That's what he does best!* Hadn't he changed enough of her life already?

The alarm clock sounded more shrill and resounding than she recalled. It was identical to the dismissal bell at school. Neala blinked a few times. Roy Wilkins stayed on stage while those on the bleachers next to her began to leave. She shook her head. It wasn't a dream. The nightmare would go on.

Neala climbed down from the bleachers as quickly as possible. She excused herself from Reganne, assured her she was still spending the night, and then made a beeline for the restroom. As she pushed her way against the flow of the exiting crowd, Neala slipped her hand into her jean pocket. She pressed a few buttons on her cell phone, starting it up by memory. Questions burned in her mind. She would make answers materialize.

Neala slipped into an empty stall. She waited until the last footfall and giggle announced that she was alone. Then, she brought out her phone and dialed the number. She waited for the ringtone, dialed in the extension, and then waited again. In a matter of seconds, a voice answered from the other end of the line.

"You have reached the offices of Hank's Pharmaceutical Supply. This is Jane O'Malley, how may I direct your call?"

Neala pressed the phone closer. "Mom, it's me."

Jane's syrupy customer service voice altered. "Oh, Neala, what a surprise. No pranks this time? Jeez, that was a short assembly."

Neala ran a hand through her hair. "Yeah, it was. Mom, listen, about the changes..."

"Yeah, what about them? Must be something big for you to call so soon. Are you still at school?"

"Um, yeah." Neala inhaled deeply. On her exhale, she let it all out. "Mom, Mr. Pierce retired and now Roy has the position of principal over Chancellor."

"Okay. That's great! I told you he got promoted."

Neala bit her lower lip. "You mean you knew? Why didn't you warn me?"

"Of course I knew. I didn't think it would be a big deal. I think I might actually convince him to tweak your grades a bit. You're still going to Reganne's. Right? Roy wanted to plan a date night since you'll be away..."

Neala closed her eyes. "Mom, please stop." Her mother stopped her chattering. Neala composed herself by opening and closing her right hand. Then, she spoke again. "It is a big deal, Mom! Having him around at school is going to be so awkward and…he's changing everything."

"Well, there's bound to be some changes…"

"No, Mom. Everything! He cancelled morning prayer. What's with that?"

There was a moment of silence on the other end of the line interrupted by nothing but the sound of typing. Finally her mother answered. "Hon, don't worry about it. Roy has problems. Goodness, do you really care that much about prayer in school?"

Neala rolled her eyes back and looked at the tiles on the ceiling. Did she? She shook her head. "I guess not. Sorry for the outburst. Look, Reganne is waiting for me. Gotta go." She frowned. "And thanks for nothing."

Neala ended the call before her mother could respond. She closed her eyes. What had she expected? Her mother could never read her anger or hurt. She stuffed her phone in her pocket. Her head fell back against the stall door. Truth was, Roy had just cancelled the most important part of the day. She could never be a religious freak and keep her image in school. Still, it was a simple fact. Prayer got each hour started off right; especially Daniel's prayer.

Neala groaned. Oh, what this must be doing to him. If she knew how, she would pray right here and now. Pray that somehow things would straighten out. Pray that Roy would regret taking the position and leave her alone. But the thought made her palms feel clammy and her throat feel as if it was coated in sawdust. Would God listen? Would it matter? She had heard of miracles but would this turn into one? Probably not, especially if God heard the message from her. So instead, Neala unlocked the stall door and walked away. Everything was different now, and nothing could change that.

✝

75

"He can't do this," said Daniel again.

Art, Sean, and Matthew sighed behind him. They were at Art's house, but their original plans had been dashed before soccer practice started. Now, they simply found the room to be a perfect solace.

Daniel had finally stopped pacing and now stared out of Art's large bay window. The heat outside was unbearable, coming toward the window in waves as if it were taunting the boys inside. They had nowhere to go but a ventilated, miserable room.

Art lay on his bed, legs crossed, looking up at a poster of the American soccer team. Sean sat on the ground across from him, shuffling a stack of Uno cards. He had begun a game of solitaire to keep from banging his fist into the wall. Matthew sketched an eerie caricature of Principal Wilkins in the left margin of his English notebook. Finally, Art sat up.

"We can't change what's happened, Daniel."

Daniel furrowed his brow. "We can fight it."

Art sighed. "Us? Coach Wilkins would never take us seriously."

Daniel didn't need him to say anything else. The betrayal they felt from the man who was supposed to help them fulfill their dreams was an unmentioned sorrow.

Daniel frowned. "Let no man despise thy youth," he whispered.

Art joined him at the window, putting his hand on his shoulder. "You know, we're lucky to have been given this opportunity for so long. This kind of stuff swept over schools ages ago. No mandatory prayer, no school funded Bible groups, nothing left in the public school system to remind kids that God is out there. Nothing to show them that He's worth living for."

Daniel hung his head. He closed his eyes, balling his hands into fists. "We have to remind them."

Sean put down his stack of cards and looked up at his two friends. "And we will," he said, "in the way we live every single day. It's more than the teaching and reaching, Daniel, it's how we live, separated from the world. That's what counts."

Daniel exhaled. Sean made sense. But couldn't they do something more? Three hundred students were now closed off from faith in God. It wasn't religion Daniel worried about; it was the personal relationship with Christ that Mr. Pierce had been trying to preserve.

Through every prayer and the Bible study, he hadn't been forcing God down their throats; he had simply been introducing Him, showing the students that He existed and He was there for them. For years God was evident in Chancellor High. When all of these signs dissipated, what would the students have? Those who knew God wouldn't lose much, but those who didn't would lose everything. And Daniel could only stand back and watch. He could imitate Christ, but would they see? Or would the faculty purposely blind the students? Anyone could be a moral person; that was how the government shut God out. Daniel shook his head. Sometimes he wished he had more influence. No matter what the Bible said, everyone belittled youth. What could they really do?

Matthew pulled away from his sketching and straightened. "Hey, we can still have the Bible study."

All eyes turned to Matthew. Daniel raised his brow as Matthew grinned. "We could have it right here. Principal Wilkins can't interfere with our evangelism outside of school. In fact, more kids might attend off campus. There's no pressure to be big in the eyes of their friends. We can turn this around right under Coach's nose."

Hope spread through Daniel and filled every heart in the room. Like a domino effect, the idea coursed through them, settling comfortably over the pit of fear threatening to swallow them. Art and Daniel grinned simultaneously. Sean stood and slapped Matthew on the back.

"Now, that's what I'm talking about, Brother! Nothing like playing your cards right. Maybe this is the break we've been waiting for." Sean glanced at Art. "Your house is the closest to Chancellor. What do you say?"

Art rubbed his jaw. Then, he winked. "I say, The Crusaders are no longer null and void."

The cloud that followed them since the assembly lifted. The first ray of sunshine escaped dread's grasp. Daniel allowed it to warm him. Maybe this storm wouldn't be so big. One thing he did know, he wouldn't give in to Coach's pressure. He wouldn't cave in on his faith. He glanced at his friends. None of The Crusaders would.

The Crusader's gathered Daniel's posters and decided what information would have to be changed. They couldn't take them on campus, but they could send them to the home addresses of their classmates. The blog would be a daily devotional spot and prayer board. For hours, they discussed the possibilities and challenges they were facing. This was a whole new ball game, but the same strategy would win over Satan's team. When 5:00 rolled around, they closed with the most familiar play of all: prayer.

Art stood and fished out his keys from his jeans. He looked at Daniel. "Come on. I'll give you a ride home."

Daniel reluctantly pulled away from his group of friends and followed Art out the door.

"See ya guys tomorrow." he called back to Sean and Matthew.

Matthew winked at Daniel. "See ya, Rookie."

Daniel punched him in the arm and then hurried to catch up to Art. Someday soon he would grow out of that nickname. He thought of his first game following the Labor Day Retreat. It would be the first soccer game in Chancellor not to be preceded by prayer. Daniel sighed as he got into Art's car. This continuance of the Bible study was a small victory. But, would it be enough?

CHAPTER 11
WATER

The saltwater sprayed Daniel in the face. The air sifted through his cropped hair and invited him to release the tensions of life. For two days, he had done just that. Carriage rides, plaza explorations, a midnight rendezvous at the pool, crowded and noisy morning devotions, and fishing from the crack of dawn until noon had made him forget what was waiting at home. Charleston, South Carolina, was warm and welcoming, even at the end of the fall season.

Daniel felt the sun beat on his back and let the warmth pound through him. He was sweating, but it felt good. He glanced at the sea below. The waters whipped around the motorboat he stood in, answering the call of the wind above. The *Raven* cut a path through the waves, gliding like the bird it was named after. Gray clouds promised a coming storm, but there was just enough time for a Low Country Boil on the beachfront. He smiled.

The ocean had grown on him. It made Matthew queasy and Art was accustomed to it; but the moment Daniel caught sight of the whitecaps, it pulled him in. Its energy swirled around him, constant and unpredictable, with a power that was both welcoming and frightening. The sea embodied its Creator, making Daniel almost envy its flow. Almost. But love did not envy.

The *Raven* neared her dock. Its motor sputtered and stopped completely. She floated the rest of the way in, carried by the water away from the water. The youth pastor tied the boat to the dock. Reluctantly, Daniel pulled away from the ocean to meet the land. The boys shoved and jumped on their way off the Raven's back. Daniel didn't follow. Art passed him, gave him a wink, and chuckled as he escaped Matthew and Daniel.

Matthew shrugged and both of them reached toward the cooler sitting between them on the waxed deck. Out of the eleven guys, they had caught the least. Therefore, the menial task of carrying their heavy catch was handed down to them. He shot the guys on shore a good-natured grin as they watched them. Some waved teasingly; some tried to hurry them; and all of them smiled in a contagious way. Daniel moved his feet a little faster, making a queasy Matthew almost trip. They all laughed. When they finally made it to the beach, the entire group heard shouts of greeting behind them.

Fifteen teenage girls, plus Mrs. Timberlake, came toward the fishermen. With flip-flops and an array of colored outfits, they stopped next to them like a rainbow coming to earth. They chattered and laughed and bravely inspected the gutted fish in the cooler. Daniel scanned the familiar faces around him, searching, knowing she was there. Mrs. Timberlake whispered something to her husband and still he searched the crowd. When their eyes met, one pair startled, the other questioning, Mr. Timberlake held up his hands for silence. Neala looked away.

"We boys are going to the house to get presentable. Our scent seems offensive to some."

Bro. Timberlake gave his wife a pointed look. Her Asian features lit up and she nodded. She declared them exiled from the beachside at present. With a full-hearted laugh, the youth pastor led his group toward their beach house.

Trinity's teens had been blessed to have been offered two adjoining beach houses on a private beachfront. The retreat's cost altered considerably with no motel involved. And having a beach all to themselves was pure luxury. The retreat that almost didn't happen had become a great blessing.

In the beach house, the guys hit the showers. Daniel waited near the end of the line. Ah, the penalty of having a bad day on the waters. When it was finally his turn, he washed off the seawater, fish guts, and putrid scent of the ocean. The ocean's bittersweet scent combined life and death swirling into a harmonious blend. It was exactly what he'd sensed in Neala's eyes moments ago. Was God in there somewhere? He felt compelled to find out, once he was presentable.

Daniel emerged from the beach house in a pair of khaki cargo pants and a white Trinity tee. The smell of frying fish permeated the air. Along with their youth group, teens from local churches milled the beachfront. Daniel's eyes searched the crowd. It had nearly doubled in size. Art, halfway through his dinner, was setting up chairs for guitarists and other musicians following the cookout. Matthew was speaking to Sarah, the youth pastor's daughter. Daniel shook his head. In a few months, they would be dating. He thought of joining them but instead veered toward the grill and a tower of paper plates. Tonight, he'd give them privacy.

He made small talk during dinner, finding an acquaintance here and there; but he never stopped searching. He couldn't understand his impulse to find Neala. Still, something kept drawing him toward her—or Someone. It made it even harder that she so easily lost herself in a crowd. It was one of the gifts he lacked but she had in great abundance.

As he wrapped up the remains of his meal and discarded it in the white trash bag on the sand, he spotted her. The sun cast red hues over the teens. Daniel straightened, seeing her for the first time since the afternoon. She withdrew from the girls in the youth group and sat a few inches away from the crowd. She was always alone.

Daniel gave himself no chance to think twice. He immediately walked toward her. She looked different tonight. Her face was almost bare of makeup; only a small coat of mascara darkened her long eyelashes, accentuating her big gray eyes. And instead of her usual shorts and tees, she was ensconced in a long, citrus orange dress with short ruffled sleeves. They looked like butterflies resting on her tan shoulders. Daniel breathed in deeply. She was beautiful. But was there something beyond her beauty? He knew there was. That was why he

81

approached her. That's why he stopped before her when her eyes turned toward him. He grinned.

"Hi ya."

Neala blinked in surprise. "Hi."

"May I join you?"

She nodded. He settled down in the sand, stretching his sandaled feet well past her bare ones. Beside him, she looked small and vulnerable.

Feeling her eyes on him, he turned. She was watching him, eyebrows raised.

"What?" he asked.

"Are you stalking me?"

Daniel almost laughed until he saw seriousness etched on her face. What kinds of things brought these assumptions to her mind? He cleared his throat. "Not a chance."

She smiled. "Good." Then added, "I knew you weren't."

Both of them faced the beachfront, watching the musicians set up for their cantata. Daniel shifted. Maybe he should have joined Sarah and Matthew. He knew them already. He took a deep breath and stilled. There was only one place to start.

"So, how was your day?" he asked.

She cocked her head. "Do you really want to know or are you just making conversation?"

"Ummm....both."

She laughed, a clear tinkling laugh that washed over him like the waves on the sea. Drawing her knees into her chest, she rested her chin on top of them. She smiled. "It was great. We went to a shopping mall, and I haggled at almost every store. I'm surprised I didn't get kicked out." She laughed softly.

He frowned. "Haggled? Why would you do that?"

"Why? Why not ask for a better price?"

He shrugged. "I guess I just trust the store owners to know what's best."

She straightened, pointing a finger at him. "See, that's where you're wrong. You've gotta know when they're charging too much and stand up for what they should be charging."

He leaned back against his arms, splaying his fingers behind him. "That's why I don't go shopping. I'd rather play sports or gut fish all day."

She wrinkled her nose. "Ugh! Guys!" She turned back to face the water. "I don't care what you say." Her voice softened. "It's the best day I've had in a long time."

He smiled. "Me too."

Silence fell over them as musicians took their places on the beachfront. It was the sort of silence that came from a tentative companionship waiting just outside life's doorstep. He smiled. He was glad he'd chosen to sit next to her on this Sunday night's worship service. Then again, maybe he hadn't been the one to choose his seat.

Soft strains of guitar music swept over the beach. Daniel recognized the song immediately. He sang along to "Holy, Holy, Holy." Neala chimed in next to him, her voice a melody in itself. She exuded music. Daniel smiled a secret smile. He'd seen a glimpse of the hidden Neala in her music. She was someone beyond the girl who was part of the school's "in" crowd. She was a girl with more questions than answers. Daniel cocked his head. One day he would tell her—but not today.

After a few more hymns and testimonies, Art stood. The diminishing sun painted shadows across the group of teens. Art announced that they would sing the last song until the sun disappeared. The crowd cheered. Then, as the other musicians found a place in the sand, Art strummed the first notes of "As the Deer." Daniel followed along, the words a balm to his soul. On the second verse, he realized there was silence next to him. He turned.

Neala wasn't singing. She stared at Art, her eyes wide and glazed over. With tears? Her chin trembled. He could feel a battle taking place by the rigid set of her shoulders. Battle against what? Daniel furrowed his brow.

"Neala?"

She jumped at the sound of his voice. She glanced at him, gasped, and shook her head. Before he could say more, Neala rose to her feet and hurried away. It happened so quickly that he had to blink a few times. No one else noticed her slip away. Had she chosen this place on purpose?

Daniel stood to his feet. He used the fading daylight to follow her small footsteps. The sand she ran over was cold from the shadows of approaching night. Daniel felt like a pursuer. But Someone told him to continue. He knew better than to fight Him. He had to find her. He did.

Neala sat on the edge of the dock with her back to him. Opposite her, the *Raven* bobbed up and down in the water. Her feet dangled over the edge of the metal dock, and she stared out at the sea as if the dock had forced her to stop. He paused. *Should I leave her alone?*

Neala sighed. "I know you're there."

Daniel froze. She scooted to her right, making room for him. After a brief pause, he joined her at the edge of the water.

She shook her head. "Are you sure you're not stalking me?"

Forced humor masked her voice. He turned his head to look at her, but she kept her gaze on the water in front of them. He swallowed. "What's wrong?"

"Water, water everywhere, not a drop to drink," she whispered.

Her voice drifted on a small breeze rising around them. He faced the ocean and waited for her to speak again. He gazed at the disturbed water, the red sky, signs of an oncoming storm. He could cope with a storm. Could she? Or was she already struggling to? He turned again and her chin trembled.

"Neala?"

"That song, it's just..." she shook her head, "...they don't know what it's like to be thirsty, not really. Not thirsty enough to pant for the unreachable."

He furrowed his brow. "Do you?"

She answered him softly, bitterly. "Yes."

She shivered. The darkening sky sent a canopy of frigid air over them. He wanted to reach for her, to offer warmth, but her stiff shoulders forbade it.

He breathed deeply. "What are you thirsty for, Neala?"

"Everything. Acceptance, love, faith..." her voice trailed off in a tremor.

Daniel picked up the unspeakable. "God?"

"Yeah, sure, I guess. Mostly God."

Daniel pointed at the heavens. "There is more water in the atmosphere than on earth. All we have to do is breathe it in." He looked at Neala as she watched the clouds drifting above them. His heart ached. *God help me.*

"God is all around us, Neala. There's no need for you to stay thirsty. He's here."

She lowered her head, tucking her chin against her chest. "With you, yes. I feel Him when you're around, and when I'm with the Timberlakes, and at Trinity. But He's not with me. He...knows better. I'm not part of the group He likes to mingle with, the chosen girls who surround me at church all the time. The guys like you. I'm...I'm too dirty."

Daniel frowned. He willed the shadows to force her gaze on him so that he could look into her eyes, declare to her all the worth hidden in her. But she continued avoiding him. He shook his head. "You're wrong there, Neala. God isn't prejudiced, and His Gift is not partial to a certain group. For God so loved the world, Neala. All of it, especially you."

"And yet His Son commanded you not to be friends with the world. You should go away. I embody the world, Daniel. You should beware being here with me."

He cocked his head, taking a deep breath to collect his thoughts. "The world is a dangerous place. He expects us to live set apart from it. But He also expects us to pull others out of it. It's like knowing your enemy's greatest disease and having the cure in your hands. We are not to partake of the world's disease but offer it Jesus' redemption."

Daniel cupped his hands together and held them beneath her lowered head. He watched her eyes focus on his empty hands. He didn't move; he just let her stare. "Christ's hands were scarred for you, Neala, and for me. My hands carry His blood because I dipped into His well of living water. He can replace the world's disease and fill you with His blood. All you have to do is accept the donation. Will you? Will you quench your thirst, Neala?"

For a moment neither of them moved. Their breaths blended in with the waves that lapped beneath their feet. Then, slowly, Neala reached out a finger toward Daniel's hands. She moved it in circular motion just inches above the ditch his palms created. Daniel wondered if she could see the pool of blood in his hands. He prayed she would jump in. A single tear trailed down her dark cheek. *Beautiful.* It landed in his hands, and he didn't draw back. Was this how God felt when He caught his own tears and those of His other children?

Neala lifted her finger and her face. She looked at Daniel. Her eyes drew him in, big, frightened, desirous eyes. But he read the answer in them and his mouth went dry.

"Maybe. Someday." She said.

Daniel's chest tightened. "You may not have someday."

She ran a hand through her hair. "I know but—no one has ever—I'm just not..." she bit her lower lip. He could see more tears forming, but she forced them down with a smile. "I'm not ready. I'm thirsty, but not ready. I think that's why I ran away. It's a scary thing for me."

Daniel wanted to push. He wanted to crush her resistance with all the willpower he had in his grasp, but he felt God's hands still him. Not everyone cracked under pressure, some melted. He couldn't let that happen to Neala. He withdrew his hands, her tear still clinging to his skin. *And of some have compassion, making a difference.* Perhaps this tear would make a difference someday. He silently offered it to God. He'd done his best. The rest was up to Him.

Neala leaned back, scanning the beachfront they had run from. "The music stopped."

He nodded. The sun was down. Night had come and morning was soon to follow. It was the way of life. Without speaking any further, they both stood and walked toward the beach houses. Daniel kept his head down, watching his sandals and her bare feet make imprints in the sand. Tomorrow their footprints would be gone, but this night would stay in his heart forever.

The crowd on the beach was thinner. The two beach houses were alive with noise and electricity. Daniel stopped in front of the girl's beach house and waited for Neala to go inside. Before she did, she turned.

"Daniel, thank you for tonight. I've never told anyone before about my struggle with God." She bit her lower lip again. "Don't take my response personally. I'm just stubborn."

He nodded. "Okay."

"And Daniel, don't stop offering your cure."

"It's not mine, Neala; it is God's."

"I know, I just mean, a lot of people need it, need Him. I'm not the only thirsty one." She smiled. "Well, good night."

Daniel mumbled a good night and watched her slip through the front door of the beach house. He broke into a cold sweat despite the cool night. Looking at his beach house a few steps away, he decided he wasn't ready for sleep...not anymore.

He walked down toward the dark beach water. The waves and wind were becoming more turbulent by the second. He slipped his feet from his sandals, watching the tide come in. Neala's words traveled with the tide, burning in his heart.

"I'm not the only thirsty one."

The cold sand shifted beneath his toes with every wave that came in. Moving, never still, a vision of three hundred students hovered behind Daniel's open eyes. Suddenly, he could see them standing in the ocean. Neala's words came back to him again and again, each time a little louder, more distinctive.

Daniel lowered onto his knees, cupped his hands again, and let the ocean's saltwater wash over them. This was the kind of water the world offered. It was sparkling, tempting, and life-taking. It would drown Chancellor. The tide was coming in, and no one could stop it—no mere youth. Daniel glimpsed Neala's face amongst the many students taking in the world's water. She smiled. *Don't stop offering your cure.*

He gasped as the waters withdrew from his hands. Masquerading as the wind, a voice he knew far too well whispered a challenge. He shivered. He fumbled for his sandals and walked to his beach house on bare feet.

God was asking him to do something big…bigger than his planned term paper, bigger than a hidden Bible study. It was something that clung to him through a sleepless night and four-hour bus ride home. Something he didn't understand. The challenge wasn't what frightened him; it was the roads it might take him down. It could lead anywhere, even to the depths of Sheol. He wouldn't dare step toward it. The world wasn't ready to follow down this path. And neither was he. After all, he was just Daniel Stevens.

CHAPTER 12
SEND

Voices rose from the overflowing bleachers lining Chancellor High's soccer field. Men in business suits, children and mothers arriving from daycare, students and alumni, and parents from both opposing teams all held their breaths as the Friday night game rose to a crescendo. A wave started and ended in the center of the stands. Chancellor's fans were enraptured with the figures running across the field. Constrained ecstasy wrapped around the spectators in a cocoon of tension. Hot dogs and cotton candy were set aside. Nails were being bitten. Hearts beat in a familiar fear that accompanied every sporting event on this field. There were fifteen minutes left. One more point would make the difference. Which team would take the field today?

Outside of the field boundaries, Daniel gripped the bench that he sat on until his knuckles turned white. His jersey was drenched in sweat. His leg and arm muscles wound tightly beneath the fabric of his uniform and his cleats dug into the ground. He watched the soccer ball roll from one of his team members' feet to the next. An opponent stole the ball, running down the field rapidly. Daniel exhaled and rubbed his face with his left hand as the Conqueror's goalkeeper, number seven, stopped the potential goal with a chest catch. A collective sigh joined in with Daniel's. The clock continued to tick, each second as important as the one before.

"Defense! Get your head in the game! Come on!"

Daniel glanced toward the end of the bench where the Conquerors' expelled captain was jumping on the balls of his feet. Elliott's face was red, his hand balled into a fist which he crushed into his other hand in frustration. The referee sent him a warning look from the field. Daniel hoped Elliott would watch his temper. He was already the cause for the Conqueror's playing with only ten members in the second half. He had way too many red cards on record.

As Elliott reduced his tirade to pacing and whispered curses, Daniel turned his attention back to the field. The Conquerors were doing well, but so were the Scorpions. Their bright red and yellow uniforms hurt his eyes and dominated the white, blue, and gold uniforms displayed by his teammates. Daniel glanced through the sheen of red and spotted number ten receive an instep pass and move the ball forward.

"That's it, Art. Stay focused. Keep control," he called out.

The ball got closer to the goal. Daniel felt as if he were on the field himself. He could see the sweat plastered on Art's face, his heaving chest, his focused eyes, and pinched brow. When Art's lungs tightened with exertion, Daniel's lungs tightened in anticipation. Inch by inch, then yard by yard, the soccer ball passed from one team member to another, moving forward past the halfway line and center circle. Art dove toward the penalty arc, waiting, receiving a push pass from Sean. Daniel stood, his heart thumping uncontrollably. It was coming. Art wasn't out of bounds. He turned the ball, the goal in plain view. Daniel nodded.

A gasp rose from the crowd as one of the Scorpions slid toward Art, his cleats connecting with Art's ankle. Art cried out, the ball sailing out of range. He fell to the ground. Rolling to his side, his hands gripped the affected bone. Daniel winced as the referee blew his whistle. A yellow card emerged and was offered to the Scorpion who caused the offense. The Conquerors raised their hands in frustration. The crowd went rampant with cries over the unethical move. Tension rose and time decreased as the coach inspected the injury.

Daniel paced back and forth, his mind reeling. Concern over his friend and the probable outcome of the game consumed him. He saw Coach Mackenzie kneeling over Art. Art shook his head, squeezed his eyes tightly, and said something indiscernible from this distance. The referee nodded a few times and motioned toward the bench. Daniel closed his eyes, clenching his fists.

Lord, do something. Don't let Art be severely injured. Turn this game around. We need a miracle on the field.

"Daniel!"

He opened his eyes to see Coach Mackenzie walking toward him. Behind the coach, a few of the team members were helping Art reach the bench. Were they going to execute a field change?

Coach Mackenzie reached Daniel's side and slapped him on the shoulder. "Rookie, take the field. You don't have time to condition, so just go do your best. Let's get this done."

Daniel nodded dumbly and reached for his shin guards. He placed them above his cleats and hopped in place for a few seconds. He was taking the field? This was his first game and Mackenzie's first display of new strategies. If he blundered, this would be the end of both of their futures. His stomach clenched and quivered at the same time. He paused for a moment, waiting for Coach Mackenzie to realize his mistake and pull out a more experienced backup. There were only five minutes in the game; they needed someone to make a difference.

"Stevens," called Coach Mackenzie, "get into action!"

Swallowing hard, he accepted a high five from Art and ran out on the field. The crowd went wild when the referee blew the whistle to commence the game. He settled in his defensive position as the left fullback. He called out to the right fullback, making sure that they were in line with one another. The ball began to move forward as the clock ticked by much more quickly than Daniel liked. He stayed in his defensive position, calling out to his teammates, his ears and eyes focused on those around him. He dodged a few Scorpions, making himself available for the ball.

The ball moved forward, but no play was enacted by the Conquerors. The Scorpions were too tight in their defense. They were determined to keep the ball away from the goal. Daniel winced as the opposing team captain stole the ball from Sean. The Scorpions came toward the goal, too close for comfort. With three minutes to go, there was only one move to make. It was a risk, but without it they would definitely lose the game.

He called out to the right fullback. When he got his attention, he clapped his hands and moved in from his outer position on the field. He shot a prayer of praise as the right fullback caught on and made his own move. It was time for the Conquerors to overlap.

The right fullback reached the Scorpion captain first, slide tackling him and snatching the ball right from under his feet. There were shouts of affirmation and advice from team members and spectators alike as number fourteen shielded the ball and turned back toward the Scorpion goal. Daniel ran forward, wide open, and receptive to the right fullback's next move. It came just as sixty seconds marked the scoreboard.

Daniel kept his foot parallel to the target. Three Scorpions were closing in on him: one defender from the right, one defender from the left, and one midfielder from behind. Daniel could smell his sweat. He could feel his breath on his neck. With his support foot pointed on the same plane with the ball, Daniel struck the final blow. The ball sailed through the air, toward the goal, skimming over the goalkeeper's fingers. Just as the referee drew his whistle to his lips, the ball hit the back corner of the net. The goalkeeper fell to the ground and the careening Scorpion midfielder tackled Daniel. The whistle sounded, signaling the end of his first game.

For a moment, the crowd went completely silent. Every eye fixed on the scoreboard. Would the impromptu goal count? Did it reach the net in time? Daniel pushed himself up on all fours, heaving, his heart in his throat. The numbers in the home box slowly changed from three to four. The Conquerors took the field!

The constrained ecstasy overflowed throughout the stands. Daniel helped the Scorpion midfielder to his feet and then turned to face his teammates. Those sitting on the bench and those who had participated on the field came toward him in an overwhelming rush. Soon, the team was a tangle of jumping legs and embracing arms. Daniel celebrated with them, shouting in unbelief. And, amidst the chaos, he closed his eyes to thank the Lord for the miracle He had granted to the Conquerors.

†

I can't believe it!

Neala rushed from the stands and through the crowds. Daniel was amazing! There had been groans all around her when Mackenzie put him on the field. Nobody knew him, nobody trusted him, and nobody wanted the rookie on the field. Even Neala had entertained doubts when Daniel took Art's place. Now, along with the rest of the crowd, she was certain that Daniel would be the next "athlete of the year" in Chancellor. Deep down, she wanted him to be.

As parents and friends assembled near their cars to wait for the team members to emerge from the locker room, Neala waited just outside the gym doors. She would usually meet Elliot here; but, maybe, just before he came out, she'd be able to catch Daniel. What would his reaction be if he heard all of the comments about him that had been thrown about in the last ten minutes? "Promising future" and "Amazing player" and "A kid with real promise."

Neala felt goosebumps on her skin. She so wanted to be the one to tell him. She wanted to see the pleasure on his face, the glint of pride in his eyes. But at the same time, she feared being the first one to see that pride. Daniel was the one guy who didn't care if she talked about deep things; he didn't take pride in his own accomplishments or thoughts above others. Neala remembered their night on the beach and a slight smile curved the ends of her lips. Maybe it wasn't the pride she wanted to see. Maybe it was the lack of it that she wanted to witness. Would her eagerness shatter the image she had of Daniel? The gym doors burst open. She took a deep breath. It was time to find out.

The Conquerors exited the double doors of the gym in a bevy of raised hands and shouts of victory. From the parking lot, parents and friends echoed their victory. Neala stepped back to let them pass. Her eyes scanned the jersey numbers, searching for twelve and five.

93

To her surprise, neither of them was present. Confused, she stepped closer to the team members and right into the back of their middle defender.

Neala stepped back, dazed for a moment by the impact. She shook her head. "I'm sorry."

Art winked and grinned. "No problem, Neala. I should've been watching those around me. All the excitement, you know."

She nodded. Art looked over his shoulder and then back at her. "Are you waiting for Elliot?"

She shifted from her left foot to her right foot. With a sigh, she nodded again. When had her waiting for Elliot become so commonplace? Why? She looked up at Art and saw the same question in his eyes. He motioned with his thumb at the gym behind them. "He's talking to Coach. They're going to be a while."

Neala bit her tongue before she asked about Daniel. What would Art think about her then? Would he warn Daniel to stay away from her? She thanked Art and made her way toward the open gym doors. At the very least, she had to wait for her ride home. She sighed as she entered the cool gym with its lines of bleachers and newly waxed floors.

The Conquerors' knight mascot stood on the far-left corner of the bleachers. She made her way toward it. She sat at the edge of the bleachers. Her hands curled around the cold metal beneath her as she stared at the armed statue. She smiled softly. If the mascot had a face, it was hidden behind the visor of his helmet like a mask of fake iron. Neala glanced into the empty eye sockets. Did this "conqueror" witness all the real difficulties that Chancellor's students faced besides sporting events? Or did his visor only encourage life's masquerade? Neala stood and walked toward the statue. She narrowed her eyes. What if she lifted the visor? What would she find? Neala raised her hand.

"That may not be wise."

She turned quickly. Her eyes widened when she saw Daniel standing only inches away from her. His scent of fresh grass and sweat surrounded her as he grinned at her.

Hi there," she said, "I was actually looking for you."

Daniel winked. He moved closer to the mascot and shook his head. "Sorry, he's the wrong height."

She shrugged. "My mistake." She took a deep breath and then released it dramatically. "You were amazing today!"

He cleared his throat. His brow furrowed. "Was I? It was a big risk, actually but..."

"I know. I haven't seen an overlap for years. Where did you learn that?"

He scratched his jaw. "My mother taught me; it was just a last resort."

She grinned. "Well, that last resort may have crowned you the most valuable player. Everyone is talking about it." Neala pointed at Mike. "You, Daniel Stevens, are a Conqueror." She cocked her head. "In many ways."

He looked at Mike reaching up to touch his helmet. Neala watched him closely. Was there pride? He whispered something to himself and then frowned. His shoulders dropped. He looked back at her and shook his head.

"I'm not the Conqueror, Neala. God was on the field."

Neala put her hands in her pockets. She thought for a moment. "Yes, I think He was Daniel. I think He was with you."

A light rose in Daniel's eyes. He glanced at Mike, the open gym doors, and the people milling about outside, and then back at Neala. He swallowed.

"Neala, do you pray?"

Neala opened her mouth then closed it. She slowly nodded. "Sometimes...at church. Why?"

Daniel exhaled. "Thank you. You have solved a very big problem for me. Neala, pray for me. Just pray. Can you do that?"

Neala smiled. "I can try."

He inhaled as if he were taking a breath for the first time in a long time. He reached out for Neala's hand and squeezed it gently. "So can I."

With no further explanation, Daniel rushed toward the end of the bleachers, grabbed his gym bag, and walked out the gym doors.

She watched him go, her heart racing. There was something going on inside of Daniel. She felt it when he grabbed her hand. It had been as if he were asking for strength of some sort.

Neala looked down at the hand he had held. She solved one of his problems? How? She glanced back at the mascot. She reached up toward the helmet and this time actually reached the top of his head. Instead of lifting up the visor, however, she simply brushed the thin metal with her fingertips. She couldn't pull off this mask anymore than she could pull off her own. Maybe that was the point. Even the greatest conquerors sometimes wore helmets with visors like masks to protect themselves. Neala looked back at the double gym doors now void of traffic. She sat down at the edge of the bleachers, placing her chin in her hands. Was Daniel wearing a mask?

†

Daniel entered his bedroom and shut the door firmly behind him. He didn't bother to turn on the light. Instead, he moved immediately toward the desk where he kept his Bible. It was open to a passage of Scripture. Had he rushed out so quickly this afternoon that he'd forgotten to take care of his Bible? Daniel didn't look at the words on the page immediately. He couldn't. He was trembling much too badly.

He sank to his knees, facing the window. With his elbows on either side of the open book, he closed his eyes and bowed his head. He didn't know exactly what to say. He just sat there, asking for strength without words. The victory of the soccer game still hung in the corner of his mind, but it was his encounter with a dear friend afterward that clung to him. It wasn't the crowds or the applause or the exhilaration that washed over him but the soft-spoken words *"You... are a Conqueror."*

Was he really? He was just Daniel. Only Daniel. He didn't want to be more. But was that really his choice? Daniel exhaled.

Show me, Lord. Teach me... Your will.

Daniel opened his eyes. There was no booming voice or whisper in his ears, but there awaited a Book beneath him. In the waning evening light, he looked down at the words before him. It was the book of Isaiah again. He smiled as he perused the passage where Isaiah called upon his unworthiness in response to a vision of the Lord. *Woe is me!* Daniel shifted. This was getting kind of uncomfortable. He read quickly over the cherubim placing the coal on Jeremiah's lips. Daniel moved his elbow to read the next verse. He blinked once, then twice. *Also I heard the voice of the Lord, saying, Whom shall I send, and who will go for us? Then said I, Here am I; send me.*

Daniel leaned back from the Bible. He swallowed hard. God's voice was softer than he remembered. *You are a conqueror. Whom shall I send...?*

Daniel whispered, "But I'm not..." he stopped. He looked down at the cleats on his feet and the soccer ball under his bed. He had been just the "rookie" on the field, but God had been there. He was just Daniel. Maybe just Daniel was okay.

He took a deep breath. "God, this is Daniel. I, well...send... send me."

CHAPTER 13
PLAYERS

Daniel stood outside Chancellor's steps. His breath came out in puffs of frost before disappearing before him. He did not go inside immediately. Instead, he paused, watching the students pour into the building. Did they realize how much had changed since the Friday before Labor Day? Did they feel the sting of separation from God?

He glanced behind him. The steeple of Trinity Baptist Church rose into the clouds while Chancellor's American flag fluttered in front of it. Daniel swallowed hard. *God, please help Chancellor. I don't know what I surrendered to last Friday. You want me to do something, but I'm not sure what. Until I find out, I'll just pray. Don't forget Chancellor. Lord, don't forget. Thy will be done.*

Still unsure as to how this day would proceed, Daniel stepped through Chancellor's double doors. At the sight of the front office, he fought the urge to walk in and demand a change in the new school policy. Daniel took a deep breath. He spotted Art, Matthew, and Sean coming in the double doors behind him. He took comfort in the light he met in their eyes and joined them. He couldn't question authority. Only God could, in His time.

As they walked toward their lockers, Daniel heard his nickname all around him.

"Good going at the game, Rookie!"

"Hey, Rookie, you rock!"

"We're going to State with you, Rookie!"

Daniel ignored The Crusaders' teasing and politely thanked his peers. Still, he was more than happy to slip into Room 101: Chemistry. He headed straight for his desk.

Students filled the seven rows of seats in the room that smelled like formaldehyde. Daniel made his way to his desk, dodging paper airplanes and stepping over numerous handbags. As he sat his books on the desktop, Daniel glanced around him. For the first time in two months, it hit him that he was smack dab in the center of the classroom. An array of individuals sat around him, laughing and talking to each other. No one seemed affected in any way by the lack of morning prayers. In fact, they seemed happy that they now had five extra minutes to socialize.

Daniel moved his books under his desk in preparation for a normal morning. From across the room, he caught sight of Crystal, a gangly and awkward junior with greasy black hair, dull blue eyes, and a wardrobe from the seventies. Daniel flashed her a smile. Instantly, she frowned, turned around, crossed her arms, and didn't look back at him again. Daniel winced.

I'm praying for you, he thought. *I wish you could see that God is still here. God, help Crystal.*

One of the senior girls reached over with the tip of her foot and knocked Crystal's books to the floor. Immediately, the room filled with peals of laughter. Art reached over and picked up Crystal's books for her. She snatched them from him, resting her chin on her desk to hide her red face. Art whispered something to her amidst the noise that made her smile. Daniel smiled at his friend. Crystal was going to find out that God was here.

When the commencement bell rang, Professor Rodney exited the lab room with his white coat on. He moved to the front of the room, placing his goggles on top of his head. Ah, yes, the sulfurous lab was today. Professor Rodney called the class to order. When they were quiet, he faced the American flag across the room, right hand over his heart. Everyone stood, copying his stance. A few of the students leaned on the edge of their desk, signaling their boredom with this morning ritual.

Daniel placed his hand over his heart. He stared at the banner of his country. The one thing that Principal Wilkins couldn't eliminate was the prayer of Daniel's heart. As his voice rose in salute to his country, his thoughts rose to his Father.

"I pledge allegiance, to the Flag, of the United States of America,…"

God, teach these students about allegiance to You. Bring every lost soul to Your feet.

"…and to the Republic, for which it stands,…"

Teach them Your ways.

"…one nation…"

Give them Your peace.

"…under God,…"

And let me remember that You never leave us alone.

"indivisible,…"

Your kingdom come,

"…with liberty and justice…"

Your will be done.

"…for all."

Amen.

Daniel sat down with the rest of the class. He took a deep breath. Chancellor was in trouble, but all he could do was take each day one step at a time and wait.

†

"Come on, Garcia; we discussed this weeks ago. Give me the money, Wimp."

Daniel paused outside the locker room. He shifted his gym bag on his shoulder. Who besides him and The Crusaders came this early to the locker room? As quietly as he could, he opened the swinging locker room door. Upon entrance, the room looked deserted. The lockers were the only things filling the space. Daniel stood in the doorway, wondering if he had imagined the voices. Just as he was about to move forward, the sound of muscle hitting metal reverberated through the room.

"What's the matter? Too lazy to fight back? Come on, you stupid Alien; your time is running out."

Daniel dropped his bag to the ground and followed the voice of his soccer captain. What was the fool up to now? As he rounded the last row of lockers, he heard a second voice joining in with Elliot's taunt. It was Randy, the right fullback that had helped him follow through to victory at Friday's game. Both of the muscled athletes stood near the end of the lockers. Cornered, their victim was the substitute goalkeeper, a short, gangly Hispanic sophomore who referred to himself simply as Garcia. Randy reached down and shoved him against the wall.

"You know what we're talking about, Garcia. We gave you a loan, and it's time to pay up."

Daniel couldn't take another moment. He approached the group. "Hey, what are you guys doing?"

Elliot turned at the sound of Daniel's voice. He rolled his eyes and motioned to Randy who turned and crossed his arms.

"Well, if it isn't the religious rookie?" Randy shrugged. "Don't worry about this. We've got the problem under control."

Daniel glanced behind Randy. Garcia cowered in Elliot's shadow, speaking to himself in Spanish. Elliot leaned in with his fist. "Hey man, we speak English in this country. If you are going to complain about responsibilities, do it in English."

Before Elliot could punch Garcia again, Daniel pushed his way between them and caught Elliot's fist. Everyone froze. Garcia looked up and gasped, waiting for the expected struggle. Daniel looked calmly into Elliot's glare.

"I think there is a better way to solve this. Don't you agree, Elliot?"

Elliot glanced at Randy. The fullback rolled his eyes and shrugged. Slowly, Elliot lowered his hand. When Daniel could breathe again, he crossed his arms and looked between the two soccer players. Garcia slowly stood to his feet behind him.

"Now, what is the problem?"

Elliot tried to shove Daniel aside, finding only a wall of determination. He shook his head. "Look, Dude; it's none of your business. He owes me money, and I need it now. He's the one who begged me to pay for his lunch last Friday."

Daniel glanced over at Garcia. The goalkeeper trainee shifted from one foot to another. "I will give you the last quarter tomorrow. I told you I will."

Randy sneered at Garcia. "Your first mistake was walking in this morning short of your debt and thinking you could leave." Randy looked at Daniel. "Move aside, Rookie."

Daniel's jaw dropped. A quarter? They were going to beat him to a pulp because of a quarter? He reached into his jeans and grabbed the quarter at the bottom of his pocket. He turned and handed it to Garcia.

"Here, it's a gift."

Garcia stared at him for a moment. He glanced at the quarter, then at the bullies who stood behind him, daring him to take the money. Hesitantly, he grabbed the coin. Nodding toward Daniel, he reached out a trembling hand toward Elliot. Then, Randy snatched the coin from the sophomore's hand. He pointed toward the exit of the locker room.

"Get out of here, you Moocher. I hope you play better today than you pay."

Garcia whispered a *gracias* to Daniel. As fast as his feet could carry him, he rushed out of the locker room. All three soccer players stood in silence until the sound of his steps faded. Elliot turned to Daniel. He could see anger simmering behind Elliot's eyes, but there also was a contemplation hovering in front of that anger. Randy watched Daniel too, his fingers absently flipping the quarter. Finally, Elliot turned his head to the direction of some nearby benches.

"Let's talk, Rookie," he said.

He sat on one of the benches and waited. Daniel took a deep breath and settled on the bench parallel to Elliot's. Randy followed, settling a few feet away from them.

Elliot scratched his chin. "You know, Rookie, you have all the makings of a great soccer player. Heck, you might even play with the pros someday." He raised his eyebrows. "Actually, Mackenzie might even sponsor you for the annual scholarship."

Garcia's face still hovered in the back of Daniel's mind as he tried to focus on Elliot's words. "Scholarship?"

Elliot nodded. "Yeah, Man. Annually, Chancellor sponsors three Conqueror soccer players to be reviewed by recruiters. They have a special assembly to decide which of the three contestants are going to get a chance for a full scholarship at a university of their choice. From there, who knows what kind of a career you might have." Elliot smiled. "Coach has already told me I'm at the top of the list but, like I said, you've got the stuff."

Daniel clasped his hands together. This was good news, but what was Elliot leading up to? He glanced at Randy who looked away, but not before shadows began forming in his eyes. Elliot spoke before he could wonder anymore about their intents.

"The only thing is, you have a few flaws that might not get you to the top. You lack a few leadership skills." Elliot pointed toward the door Garcia had run through. "You can't be siding with freaks like that. Garcia, well, he's going nowhere fast."

Daniel stiffened. Had Elliot not seen how quickly the kid could block a goal? He shifted in his seat. He was about to speak up in Garcia's defense when Elliot held up his hand.

"I know, you're a religious freak and all, but sometimes you have to lay your soft heart aside. Yeah, we were bruising him up a little, but that's what leaders do. Coach Wilkins taught me well. He told me that if I wanted something I had to trample whatever was in my way to get it. Garcia, he's no threat. He's just a strength builder. He and the lower classmen get beat up a few times just so they know that we're in charge." Elliot leaned forward. "You love soccer, don't you, Rookie?"

Daniel raked a hand through his hair. "You know I do, but God says in His Word..."

Elliot shook his head. "No, Daniel. There is no room for buts or God if you want to play professionally. Beat down what's in your way and play with what's not." He winked and stood. "Just as long as you understand, Rookie. You'll catch on. I can tell you're real smart."

Before Daniel could respond, Randy and Elliot were walking out the door. Their confident laughter echoed with their steps. He glanced down at his number nine jersey. *There is no room for God if you want to play professionally.*

Daniel rubbed his face. He did want that scholarship. He did want to play professional soccer. He envisioned Garcia's face. What would he be doing at home right now? Would he ever get this sort of chance? Daniel clasped and unclasped his right hand, watching the muscles of his arm flexing up and down. God had given all of the Conquerors so much strength. They were the undefeated soccer team in all of Georgia. People were talking about the team being sponsored for State this year. What would he use his strength for?

Daniel stuffed his soccer jersey back into his bag. The team would file in for practice any minute now. He took a deep breath.

God, I really would love to have that scholarship.

He opened his eyes. A slow smile crept to his lips. No room for God in soccer? No prayer in Chancellor? Daniel closed his eyes again. Before the team members arrived, he prayed for each of them by name. He asked for protection in tomorrow's game. Then, he prayed specifically for Garcia, that God would work in his life and that Daniel would be more of a testimony to him.

When he was done, he looked around the locker room. Perhaps this was what God was asking him to surrender to. If no one else was going to pray, he would. And if God gave him the scholarship, he was determined to show the world just how much God could work in the soccer arena. Daniel stood from the benches. He made his way to his locker. Just before he opened his bag, he paused, grabbed a sticky note from the bottom of his pencil bag, and walked back over to Garcia's locker. With his pen, he wrote a simple message on the sticky note.

I'm praying for you.

He placed it on the inside of the locker. When he closed it, he took a deep breath. He would not become the kind of soccer player Elliot said he needed to be to succeed. He was God's soccer player.

CHAPTER 14
CROSSING

Daniel, Art, Sean, and Matthew rounded the neighborhood's last corner and headed back toward the main street. Their labored breaths mingled together as they finished the last stretch of their daily run. Every moment counted as they approached their final game of the season.

Daniel caught sight of Chancellor a few feet ahead of them. From this far away, the building looked small rather than imposing. Who would have supposed that in only a few hours this brick building would determine the future of three soccer players?

"Hey," said Art beside him, "are you ready for the big announcement?"

Daniel emitted a ragged breath as he responded. "What do you mean?"

Matthew spoke up behind them, his breath just as short as Daniel's. "Aww, come on, you know you're going to be one of the scholarship candidates."

"It's what you've been praying for, right?" added Sean.

Daniel didn't respond, but he smiled and nodded. Yes, it was one of the many things he'd been praying for. Yet, little had changed. They were still the only four Crusaders in the Bible study.

Daniel wiped his brow as they neared the gate that closed off Chancellor's soccer field. The locked chain fence was their finish line. Daniel could see their water bottles sitting by the gate. He was more than happy when they reached their destination, and he felt the cold water bottle in his hands. He sipped the water slowly, feeling his heartbeat lower, and thinking about Monday. What if he didn't get the scholarship nomination? He shook his head, droplets of sweat falling away like his doubts. He had to focus on playing hard for his last senior game. If nothing else, he would play his part in the Conqueror's last victory.

Art nudged Daniel in the side. "Don't worry. I'm sure Chancellor's secret prayer warrior will be praying for you."

Daniel smiled and took another sip of water. All of the Conqueror soccer players and a few of the students recently found numerous sticky notes in lockers and notebooks from an anonymous prayer giver. Daniel swallowed his water and capped the bottle. Sometimes it just helped people to know that someone was praying. It did hurt at times, though, when Daniel found a few of the prayer notes in the trash. Yes, the prayer warrior definitely would be praying on Monday.

As Daniel bent down to grab his gym bag, Sean pointed across the soccer field.

"Hey, I thought only the janitors and staff were allowed on the soccer field."

Daniel turned to where he was pointing. On the far end of the bleachers sat an old man in a polo and jeans. Daniel squinted. From this distance, it was hard to tell who he was. Matthew stood next to Daniel and shaded his hands, leaning over as far as his long torso would allow. He raised his eyebrows.

"It's Mr. Pierce."

Daniel furrowed his brow. What was Mr. Pierce doing on the soccer field? The elderly man sat motionless, his head hanging down, his hands clasped, and his shoulders slumped. Art patted Daniel on the shoulder.

"Come on, he's probably just reminiscing about his time at Chancellor. Retiring is always hard for old people."

Daniel picked up his belongings and followed The Crusaders toward Art's jeep. While waiting for the walkway light to give them clearance, Daniel glanced back at the field one more time. This time, Mr. Pierce's head was lifted. He was looking directly at The Crusaders. Daniel turned; the walkway light gave them the go ahead. As he crossed the street, Daniel made a mental note to add Mr. Pierce to his prayer list.

†

"Hi ya!"

Neala looked up to find Daniel looking down at her. She quickly shoved the envelope in her hand down to the furthest recesses of her purse as she got to her feet.

"Hey."

Daniel looked around. Church members mingled with each other in the background. From the corner of her eye, she saw Art, Sean, and Matthew talking to some of the guys from the youth group while keeping a curious eye on Daniel. Neala gave him her full attention. Maybe then he would go away and not cause Reganne to ask her annoying questions.

"Are you leaving soon?" he asked.

She smiled. "Yep. I'm just waiting for Elliot."

He nodded, flipping open the cover of his Bible. "Then I won't keep you long. I just wanted to give you this."

Neala watched him warily, her eyes flipping back and forth from the parking lot to the young man standing before her. He slid a piece of folded paper from beneath his Bible cover. He handed it to her. She threw her purse across her shoulder and unfolded the paper. An interesting design, consisting of the Holy Grail, a Bible, and an array of faces met her eyes. The headline, however, was what caught her attention. Her heart skipped a beat. The Crusaders? But Roy...then she saw a house address on the bottom of the page: Art's house.

She looked up at Daniel. "What is this?"

"I thought you might like to learn more about Jesus. You know, the cure. Call it a spiritual clinic. God has been burdening my heart to invite you for months now. Join us one day."

Neala refolded the poster. She took a deep breath, closed her eyes, and then lifted them toward Daniel's. His gaze was deep and bottomless, reserved and inviting at the same time.

"Daniel, what are you doing?" She whispered.

Daniel scratched his chin. "I don't know, but God does."

She cocked her head. "Aren't you afraid of what might happen if Roy, I mean, Principal Wilkins, finds out that y'all still have a Bible study?"

Daniel placed his hands in the pockets of his slacks. He gazed across the parking lot as a familiar blue sedan drew close to the church.

"I respect Principal Wilkins' decision to cancel the Bible study on campus. I don't agree with it, but I have to believe that God let this happen for a reason. Off campus, however, I'm subject to God's authority. Principal Wilkins is daily in my prayers; and, for his sake, I hope that God does not abandon Chancellor." He looked back at Neala. "If Principal Wilkins hadn't canceled The Crusaders, we would not have this outreach opportunity. I know God is at Chancellor. We just have to look harder."

Before Neala could respond, she heard Elliot honking the horn of his sedan. The other church members frowned, watching the teen-driven vehicle with caution. She folded the poster and began stuffing it in her purse.

Daniel smiled. "Think about the Bible study, Neala."

"Thanks, Daniel," she said as she began walking off of the curb, "but I don't think you want me ruining your Bible study."

He shrugged. "God wants you at the Bible study and so do I."

Neala gripped her purse strap, turning away from him. Her heart skipped as she drew closer to the sedan that pulsed with rap music playing on its stereo. *God wants you at the Bible study.* Neala shook her head. Daniel was doing a good thing and would touch many people, but not Neala Baptiste. She already went to church on a weekly basis. That was enough for now.

Neala tried to push aside her conflicting thoughts about the Bible study. She climbed in next to the gang and pressed up against the shoulders of the people who were familiar to her. Throughout the day, Neala enjoyed her life, her way. Slowly, the invitation became forgotten, somewhere at the bottom of her purse, along with the message written on the back.

✝

Pastor Moore pressed his forehead against the cool oak of his desk. How could another week have gone by so quickly? He glanced at the notes scattered across the desktop but did not move to gather them. Attendance was low again today. Low in Spirit, too. His own heart had moved him to the altar, but he'd been the only one. Daniel, one of the newest members of the church, was at the altar almost every week.

Pastor Moore sighed and lifted his head. Ah, but it had been encouraging to see the young man reach out to the youth group outcast—the French girl; her name was Neala if he remembered correctly. Although she participated in almost all the church functions, she fellowshipped with very few, very little. Then, she was off in that blue sedan.

Glancing at his wristwatch, Pastor Moore pushed back his chair. Dinner was in fifteen minutes. He grabbed his suit jacket, tucked his Bible under his arm, and moved toward the door. As he turned off the light switch, he sighed. Tonight, he'd have to spend extra time in the Psalms. How was he to keep up the spirit when so little was happening in the lives of God's people? As he shut the door behind him, a bright yellow patch next to his nameplate made him pause. Pastor Moore raised his eyebrows. With his free hand, he peeled the yellow sticky note off his door. He read the simple phrase scrawled across the paper.

I'm praying for you.

Pastor Moore smiled. He opened the cover of his Bible and pasted the note inside. He looked at it for a moment. That is how he was to keep up the spirit. Somewhere in his congregation, someone was praying for him. Someone took note of the man of God and gave him the mercy of a prayer. Pastor Moore closed his eyes.

Lord, make me faithful in this ministry. Lord, give me strength in these hard times. Help me to keep my hope in You. Thank You for this prayer giver. Amen.

Pastor Moore gently closed his Bible. With an extra spring in his step, he walked down the church hallway singing the sweet refrains of "What a Friend We Have in Jesus." God had things under control. All Pastor Moore had to do was preach and wait.

CHAPTER 15
ADJUSTMENTS

Neala sat across the dinner table, watching warily as her mom reached over to squeeze her hand.

"I have some big news," said Jane.

Neala narrowed her eyes. "How big?"

"Well, it's going to change a lot of things…" Jane shook her head, red hair bouncing across her forehead. "First things first. The big news is," she took a deep breath, "Roy and I are engaged."

She swept her left hand from under the table to show off a new engagement ring glittering against her skin. Her mother's smile was lost on Neala. Her heart sank. "Engaged?"

"Yes! We've been talking about it for a while…"

"Whoa! A while? How long? Why didn't you ever ask me about this?"

Jane hesitated, then shrugged. "I guess I got caught up in the dreaming of it." She patted Neala's hand, moving on as if her words didn't matter. "Now, as for the changes…Roy is going to be around a lot more and you know the whole God thing makes him uncomfortable."

Neala stiffened. *I don't like where this is going.*

"So," continued her mother, "we both decided that it's best if you stop going to church. After all, it will give us all more time to spend together on the weekends."

Neala jumped to her feet. "What? Are you kidding?!"

The excitement on Jane's face disappeared. She frowned. "It's going to happen eventually anyway. Once we're married and he's under the same roof…"

"Then don't marry him!"

"Neala…"

"No! I should have a say in this! Don't give me that stupid line about spending time together as a family. I'd rather spend my time in a den of lions."

"That's enough, Neala Baptiste. It's been decided. We're getting married and, as of today, you will no longer step foot in Trinity."

"You wanna bet?"

"Neala, don't…"

"I like church. The people there care about me and God may still seem far away, but at least He's there."

"I care…"

"Don't!" Neala held up her hands and grit her teeth. Her heart pounded in her ears. "I'm so sick of lies."

A silence filled the space between mother and daughter. Before anything could bridge the gap, Neala ran to her room. Her mother didn't follow. She slammed the door as loudly as she could, locked the door, and let out a scream. Curse Roy and his lingering presence. Curse her mother for letting him in. Curse her father for leaving Jane to this life. Curse the world for desecrating the lesser things that didn't matter. Things like her.

Neala groaned. She stomped once then threw herself on her bed belly first. She buried her face in her pillows, punching them for good measure. Did Roy enjoy taking the good away from people? Did God? First her mother, then Chancellor, now Trinity. When would it end?

Neala went limp as the anger drained from her body. She turned onto her side, facing the wall. She wouldn't go back to church, that much was certain. She couldn't fight anymore.

Run!

Neala shook her head at the thought. There was nowhere to run. Besides, she wouldn't leave her mother here with Roy prowling around. Jane was weak, probably weaker around men. She needed someone to lean on, and while Neala did her share of shouldering after each break up, Jane preferred male shoulders. Had her father facilitated strong shoulders? Yes, Neala was sure of it. And he had left them to her.

Neala snatched a nearby teddy bear and cuddled him under her arm. That's what she craved. Affection without expectations. Comfort. But in this household, with its locked doors and loud voices, she had a feeling that might never come. And outside? The streets of urban Georgia were bereft of cuddling teddy bears. Here she was safe; comfortless, but safe.

But I will leave behind a Comforter...

Neala closed her eyes. She pressed the stuffed bear closer. Maybe that was what she wanted in Trinity and youth night and beach retreats. She was so close to finding it, too. In the sanctuary of Trinity, she had been closer to God than anywhere else, but no more. Would she ever feel His presence again?

The sound of Neala's ringtone made her jerk. She rolled onto her back and scooted off the bed. Instead of taking the time to search her crammed purse, she dumped all of its contents onto the floor. Her cell phone blinked red with an incoming call. She picked it up, along with a miscellaneous paper that caught her attention. Was it one of her many to-do lists? She flipped open her phone.

"Hello? Oh, hey, Reganne."

She cradled her phone between her shoulder and ear and picked up the paper lying in front of her knees. She was probably going to throw it away, but her penchant for knowing what she discarded overcame her. She began unfolding it.

"Yeah, fine. Just had another fight with Mom." Neala snorted when Reganne made a comment about lame parents. "You have no idea."

Neala decided to avoid the question about the quarrel's subject matter. Instead, she questioned Reganne about the impromptu call. Soon, her ears filled with details about Reganne's preceding date. Some football star from a neighboring college had taken her to the theater yesterday afternoon. While she listened, Neala straightened out the piece of supposed junk on her lap. She laughed at one of the cliché pick-up lines Reganne had endured. Her eyes fell on the burst of color on the inside of the paper and she froze.

The Crusaders. How could she have forgotten? She read the address at the bottom of the page. It was in walking distance from the school...every day at 7:00 in the morning. Neala glanced at her cracked window. Sanctuary.

"Neala?"

She jumped at the sound of Reganne's voice. She shook her head, noticing for the first time how her temples were throbbing. She clutched her cell phone. "Hey, Reganne, I have a killer headache. I know. Can you tell me tomorrow? Okay. See ya."

She pushed the end button. Trinity was over, but now this poster was here before her. It was a personal invitation, Daniel's invitation. Coincidence? No. God? She bit her lower lip. It could be done. She just had to find a reason to leave early in the morning. With Roy stopping by, her mother would be oblivious to her presence anyway.

At the sound of footsteps, Neala shoved the contents on the floor back into her purse. She rose to her feet and tucked the poster behind the cover of *Les Misérables,* which she kept under her pillow. It was her way of keeping a good friend nearby.

Neala sat on the edge of the bed and waited. The shadows of Jane's feet stopped under her doorway. Neala clutched the edge of her mattress. Perhaps, tonight, her mother and she would make peace. Perhaps Jane would take the opportunity to break down the door between them. Slowly, the shadows withdrew from her doorway. She exhaled. She expected too much.

Neala changed into her pajamas, flipped off the lights, and buried herself under her thin sheets. The bulk of Victor Hugo's literary work felt really good beneath her. It was solid, firm, and sure. Most importantly, it now held a secret. She glanced up at the ceiling. She felt the urge to pray. Could she be as bold as Daniel? What would it be like to take a step toward God? What if she reached for His open hands? *Someday.*

Neala's fingers searched the darkness for a discarded teddy bear. She found it and brought it to the crook between her neck and chest. She sighed. Maybe God could read the intents of her heart. He was supposed to be good at that. She closed her eyes. This was one place where a thousand Roys couldn't interfere.

†

Daniel winced. He readjusted the ice pack on his knee and returned his attention to the game. No one had scored yet. Both the Scorpions and the Conquerors were determined to keep the offense at constant odds with the defense. This had been one of the most brutal and unsuccessful games he'd ever seen.

He leaned forward on his good knee. He should be out there! Sean lost another chance to score. A collective groan swept across the field. Daniel shook his head. The Scorpions had one extra game advantage. If no one scored, they would be going to State and the Conqueror's would be left as the "almost" team. Daniel shifted, pain shooting through his left knee.

He glanced over at the Conqueror's goalkeeper. Hank groaned and hung his head over his knees. He probably wanted to be on the field as much as Daniel. A shout from the crowd shifted Daniel's attention. His heart caught in his throat as one of the Scorpions broke through the Conqueror's defense.

"Garcia!" Daniel screamed at the top of his lungs, "Stay strong, Man. Stay strong!"

Garcia lunged for the soccer ball as it approached the net, barely deflecting the goal. Daniel wiped his brow. Now all they needed was a miracle. Dread washed over him as one of the most awkward freshmen gained possession of the ball. The stands were filled with shouts of dismay. On the benches, the team members cursed under their breaths.

Daniel closed his eyes. He bowed his head and began to beg for God to take the freshman and give him the ability to score this winning touch. He didn't open his eyes, not even when he heard the crescendo of the crowd's excitement and felt the team members rise to their feet. It was not until the whistle blew and the team members began shouting, "We won!" that Daniel opened his eyes.

Then, he jumped to his feet with the team. He held out his hand as the teary-eyed freshman ran toward the benches, the gleam of victory shining in his eyes. Daniel gave him a high five and then turned to embrace Art, Sean, and Matthew. They jumped up and down. The Conquerors were going to State; and Daniel knew, without a doubt, that God was going with them. He had granted them another victory.

†

The static air in the locker room made Daniel's hairs stand on end. For an hour now, they had celebrated their victory as a team. Daniel had never signed so many jerseys in his life. Although he adamantly declined an invitation from the seniors to meet at a local hang out after the locker room celebration, he had called his guardians and asked them to prepare a small pizza party for the abstinent team members.

While adrenaline pumped continuously through Daniel's veins, he made a point to congratulate Garcia and the freshman victor one more time. As the excitement shifted to plans for the rest of the night, he noticed Mackenzie duck into his office. Daniel swallowed a gulp of soda. The nervousness he'd felt all weekend came rushing back to him. He almost had forgotten about the scholarship.

Coach Mackenzie blew his whistle to get the boys to lower the volume. A few of the most boisterous team members blatantly mocked his attempt, but Daniel leaned over and warned them to quiet down. Other team members backed him up, obviously aware of what was to come. Daniel took a deep breath. There were a total of twelve seniors on the soccer team. Each of them turned his attention toward the coach. Coach Mackenzie cleared his throat.

He beamed at the Conquerors. "Today, the Conquerors crushed the Scorpions."

The Conquerors whooped in response. Daniel winked at the freshman who was getting much of the glory tonight. Beside him, Garcia rolled his eyes.

Mackenzie held up his hands. "I'm so proud that all of you have worked together to bring us to State. This is our final game of the season until we start again in March to get in shape for the tournament on May 6. Today, I am proud to uphold a tradition that was started years ago." Mackenzie held up three folders and then laid them in his palms. "There are twelve seniors in this room. Although we hope to see all of you again as we train for State, this is officially your last game. For three of you, however, this day is also going to be a turning point for your soccer career. I have chosen three of you for the Conqueror scholarship. These choices were made based on leadership qualities, academic excellence, and skills of the game. I believe these three young men will represent our school well this summer. Now, it's time to add to your celebratory mood."

Nervous laughter filtered throughout the room. Daniel took a deep breath and held it. *God please.*

"Our first two scholarship contenders are Hank Heissman and Randy Alder."

A cheer rose from the two seniors. Randy gave Elliot a high five and then sneered at Hank. The injured goalkeeper shrugged and crossed his arms but grinned at the same time. Daniel leaned over and slapped them both on the back. He caught sight of Elliot.

The team captain's words from the first time Daniel had heard about the scholarship came back to him. *Coach already told me I'm on the top of the list.* Elliot shrugged and held up his palms. Daniel swallowed hard. He looked away from Elliot and back to Mackenzie. It would only be appropriate that the feisty team captain be the top contender for the scholarship. Daniel fought against a feeling of disappointment. He had prayed for God's will, after all.

"The last contender for the scholarship is Daniel Stevens."

Daniel stopped breathing for a moment. The whole room stilled. Every eye shifted between Daniel and Elliot. Elliot rose from his place next to Randy and pushed his way to the front.

Red-faced, he stopped next to Daniel. "Hey, the team captain is supposed to get priority. Wilkins told me I was going to get my chance!"

Mackenzie looked down at Elliot. "You did, Elliot, but Daniel is a better candidate. This is his chance now."

Elliot glared at Daniel. He winced at the disappointment in Elliot's eyes. Attempting a smile, he held out his hand. "Sorry, Man. I'm sure you'll get another chance."

Elliot stared at Daniel's outstretched hand. For a second, he made a motion as if to reach for it. Then, he spat on the ground next to Daniel's feet. Without a second glance at Daniel or anyone else in the room, Elliot grabbed his soccer gear and rushed out of the locker room with Randy right behind him. A string of curses followed in his wake. Daniel watched him go with a feeling of dread. There was someone else he would have to pray for tonight.

"Rookie, Rookie, Rookie, Rookie…"

The chant began somewhere from the back of the locker room and then rose all around him. Daniel shook his head at the attention. He beamed at Sean, Art, and Matthew who circled around him, slapped him on the back, and offered him fist bumps. They made a mock toast with their soda cans and then laughed. As the locker room gathered around Daniel chanting and cheering, he bowed his head in the midst of the celebration.

Thank You, God. And thank You in advance for whatever Your plans are with this scholarship.

Daniel smiled. God's rookie was going to show the recruiters Who God was.

†

Elliot stomped down the stairs. He walked toward the couch, searching for his game controller to the gladiator video game, and settled next to Randy. His friend gave him a sideways glance.

"Sorry about the scholarship, Elliot."

He shook his head. "No, Daniel's going to be the one who's sorry. He had no right to take my scholarship from me. I've been training too long and hard for it. One way or another, I'm going to get in." Elliot chose his player and then skimmed the choices for the arena. He clicked on the one that gave the loser to the lions in the coliseum. "I just don't know how he did it."

Randy shifted in his seat next to him. He cleared his throat. "Well, he's a religious rookie. Maybe he prayed hard enough."

Elliot glared at Randy. He clicked the start button to keep himself from slapping his friend across the face. "Don't you dare credit this to God, Randy. Keep your mouth shut."

Elliot shook his head. No, he refused to believe that Daniel's God was the One Who had handed him the scholarship opportunity. He was just too full of rotten luck. Something Elliot never had. At least not yet, but things could change in an instant with a little bit of muscle and willpower. He swerved the controller, focusing on his opponent. Elliot narrowed his eyes. With all of the vehemence he could muster, he pummeled his technological opponent to the ground. He had blue eyes like Daniel.

CHAPTER 16
SURFACING

Daniel waved at Aunt Lisa and turned to walk up Art's driveway. He stifled a yawn. He had finished his term paper just in time for the first scholarship prep practice that would begin today. He would have one less thing to think about as he worked for his dream.

Daniel paused before Art's door and shifted his backpack. He glanced at the cars parked in the driveway. Art's Jeep Wrangler, Sean's blue Cadillac, and Matthew's Volkswagen lined up behind each other. He sighed. The Crusader blog was a success, but not their attempt to grow as a study group. Daniel rapped on Art's door. Some things never changed.

The door swung inward. Art looked at Daniel, his eyes shining with contagious excitement.

Daniel grinned. "Sorry I'm late. I finished the term paper last night."

Art nodded. "It's fine, we haven't started yet anyway. We had a little surprise today."

He paused while shrugging off his jacket. "Surprise?"

Art stepped aside. "See for yourself."

Daniel stepped through the doorway, placing his backpack on the floor just inside. What had gotten Art so excited that he'd be willing to delay the Bible study for a few minutes? Daniel entered the living room. He stopped in his tracks just under the dining archway. His heart leapt to his throat.

Across from the couch that Sean and Matthew sat on, the surprise sat licking her fingers as she finished her last bite of a sticky cinnamon bun. She looked up, her gray eyes lighting when she caught sight of him.

She held up a wrinkled piece of paper. "You never said you'd be offering breakfast at the spiritual clinic."

Daniel laughed and shook his head. "That would kind of defeat the Bible study incentive." He smiled. "I'm glad you finally made it, Neala."

She glanced down at the Bible in her lap. "Me too."

After settling down in the living room with his other friends, Daniel took out the outline he'd prepared for today. It was about God's miracle performed on the blind man. As they opened their Bibles in unison, warmth flowed through him. This just might be the beginning of an answer to prayer.

†

Daniel pulled out his number nine jersey. He took a long gulp from his water bottle and glanced at the wall clock. He winced. He was barely on time. Taking a deep breath, he pulled his jersey over his undershirt. This was the day. The three scholarship recruiters were here, taking the first skills review of the Conqueror's scholarship contestants. They had been training for three weeks and still Daniel's muscles ached at the thought of all that their professional level practice entailed.

He glanced behind his shoulder and saw Hank's things already on the bench in front of his locker. He and Randy were probably waiting on the field. Taking a deep breath, Daniel shoved his water bottle in his locker. He couldn't be late, but first things first. Daniel kneeled beside the locker bench. He closed his eyes.

God, use me on the field today. Help me to play my best for You, not just the recruiters. These human judges are going to be adding a lot of pressure

124

on us today, but help us to stay focused and steady. Lord, guide me and my other Conqueror contestants. In Jesus name, Amen.

Daniel finished his prayer and looked up at the clock. He had one minute to get on the field. Tightening his cleats, he walked toward the field door. There was no need to panic. The training schedule would be strenuous and the graders harsh, but Daniel knew he could do it. He pushed open the door and walked out onto the field of his dreams.

One hour later, the three boys trudged back into the locker room. Each chest heaving, each body covered in sweat. Daniel stayed behind Hank, ever vigilant as the limping goalkeeper walked back toward his locker. When he slipped, Daniel grabbed him under his arm and led him to the bench in front of his locker. Hank winced as he stretched his swollen ankle. It didn't look good. Coach Mackenzie came behind Daniel with an ice pack in his hands. He patted Daniel on the back.

"Okay, Rookie, I've got it from here. Go ahead and get ready to head on home."

Hank looked up at Daniel and sneered. "You've done your good deed for the day, Rookie."

Daniel nodded. "You're welcome, Hank."

Hank didn't respond but instead got out his iPod. Daniel shrugged and walked back to his locker. He found Randy stuffing his gym bag with sweaty practice clothes. He smirked at Daniel when he walked in. He ignored Randy and opened his own locker. As he reached for his change of clothes, Randy rolled up his jersey and threw it at Daniel's turned back. He turned to face him.

Randy crossed his arms. "You know, Rookie, the recruiters were here today."

"Yeah. So?"

"Hank's mistake could have given you a lead in the scholarship." Randy leaned forward, his elbows resting on his thighs. He narrowed his eyes. "Why did you help him?"

Daniel sighed. He knelt down to grab Randy's jersey. "It was the right thing to do."

Randy shook his head. He snatched his jersey from Daniel's outstretched hand. "You're always doing that, Man. The right thing. Why?"

Daniel crossed his arms. He draped his jersey over his neck and leaned against the locker behind him. "Love the Lord your God with all your heart...and love thy neighbor as thyself. That basically sums it all up. I don't do the right thing for me or to show off." Randy looked away from Daniel as he continued speaking. "I do it to please my Father..."

"Your Heavenly Father. Right? You're a Christian. Right? One day you accepted Jesus as your Saviour and, now, you do everything to please Him. Right?" Randy glanced up at Daniel. "Am I right?"

He raised his left eyebrow. "Exactly."

Randy shrugged. "Don't look too shocked that I know the answer. I...I did the same thing, became a Christian and accepted Christ as my Saviour. When I was ten, actually."

Daniel blinked a few times. Randy? The bully Randy who went out drinking with Elliot every Friday? Randy was a Christian? Randy laughed nervously, glancing around the locker room. He scratched his chin and returned his gaze to the jersey in his hands.

"I've just never told anyone," he admitted. Randy frowned.

Daniel moved from the locker to sit next to him.

Randy shot him a sideways glance. "Actually, I did tell my parents. My dad was an evolutionist and my mom was an atheist at the time, but we went to a Catholic church to make it look good. I had been sneaking out of mass for two years to go with one of my friends to a small Baptist church. They always had lots of things for us kids to do, good things. During a revival one May, I felt God tugging on my heart. I was ready to believe all that I had heard about Jesus, so I met the children's minister at the altar and accepted Christ as my Saviour. It was the most amazing feeling in the world. I wanted to share it with somebody. I figured my parents would understand Heaven."

Randy shook out his jersey. He laid it across one of his thighs. "My mom slapped me across the face, and my father was furious. They told me to counsel with our family priest about the impossibility of having an assurance of Heaven. I did, but nothing that priest told me could shake my confidence in my faith. My parents, well, they never let me talk to my neighbor again. After their reactions, I promised myself I'd never share my faith again, with anyone. It wasn't worth the trouble." Randy sighed. "Then I came to Chancellor. I found my place on the soccer team, found a friend in Elliot, and freedom in popularity; and I never thought twice about my faith." Randy fumbled with his jersey. "Until I found a prayer note in my locker."

Daniel shifted in his seat. He met Randy's troubled gaze. "You didn't think your faith was important. Why?"

He shrugged. "It's easier to conform than to fight."

"Do you still think faith is unimportant?"

Randy glanced around again as if to assure himself that no one else was listening. He closed his eyes. "After I found the prayer note, I started rethinking the faith I buried. I found an old Bible in the bottom of my drawer and began reading in the Gospels."

Daniel nodded. "And what did God tell you in the Gospels?"

Randy opened his eyes. Tears rimmed the edges. "He told me that I've been real selfish, that I had wasted all of the blood Christ poured on Calvary by hoarding it all to myself. He told me again about the story of salvation." Randy wiped his eyes. "Last night I read about the parable of the prodigal son. Then, I went to The Crusaders blog and saw the same passage of Scripture posted. I took the hint. I rededicated myself to Christ…and told my parents again. This time my mother just rolled her eyes. My dad didn't answer his cell phone." Randy lifted pleading eyes to Daniel. "The only thing is, now I'm terrified, Daniel. I don't really know how to be a Christian. I am so comfortable with the walls I've built around myself at Chancellor and with my friends that I don't know where to start. How does a prodigal son start rebuilding a relationship with his Father?"

Daniel bit his lower lip. He looked straight into Randy's eyes. "The best way to do it is to allow God to place His robe over you through His Word. Search the Scriptures. Start attending a Bible-believing church. And always, always pray. Ask God to show you what to do next."

Randy cleared his throat. "I think I can do that."

Daniel smiled. "Do you mind if I pray with you right now, to get you started?"

He nodded. "It's kind of weird; I'm not going to lie, but I would like that, yes."

With Randy, the one soccer player he never thought he'd be counseling in matters of God, Daniel bowed his head in the locker room. He cleared his throat. "Lord, thank You for giving us this moment to talk about You. Thank You for bringing Randy home."

"I'm sorry, God," whispered Randy. "I'm sorry I've been running from You all these years. Forgive me for my cowardice. Give me courage to pick up my walk of faith. Amen."

For a moment, they both sat in silence. Daniel felt the Holy Spirit settle around the locker room. He smiled. What a strange place for Him to be. With a sigh, Randy straightened and opened his eyes. Daniel nodded, punching him in the shoulder.

"Now, stop holding out on your other Christian siblings, all right?"

Randy laughed. He nodded before rising to his feet. He took a deep breath. "Thanks, man, for listening and praying and stuff, and for always doing the right thing, as annoying as it might get sometimes."

Daniel laughed. "That's what brothers are for."

Randy nodded and gathered his stuff. He went to check on Hank, leaving Daniel on the far side of the locker room alone. Daniel listened to the murmur of the voices in the distance. He mulled over Randy. How many more Christians had been rebuffed and then forgotten their faith? This prodigal son had come home, but how many others would never be led back because Christians were hiding? The muscle in Daniel's jaw twitched.

God, please help all of your prodigal children.

†

Neala placed her hand over her abdomen. She had never laughed so hard in her life. Gulping in breaths of fresh air, she pulled herself off from the carpeted floor to a sitting position. Reganne followed her lead, sweeping her hair out of her face.

"It was hysterical!" she exclaimed.

Neala groaned. "Stop, I can't take it anymore."

Reganne nodded. She let a small giggle escape and then conceded. "Me neither."

Reganne jumped to her feet. She propped herself onto Neala's bed, pulled up her tanned manicured feet, and sighed. "So, are we still holding our annual party?"

Neala barely omitted a groan. She had completely forgotten about Reganne's annual winter party to finish off the soccer season. She'd stuffed the flyer into her *Les Misérables* book along with The Crusaders poster. She swallowed hard, leaning against her headboard. "I don't know, Reganne. It's on the scholarship night and with Mom being engaged to Roy, well, they kinda expect me to be there."

Reganne wrinkled her nose. She wriggled her toes and shook her head. "So, play off your Mom's emotions and find a way out. She's been acting super guilty since she threw that news on you. It shouldn't be that hard. Elliot didn't get the scholarship so maybe just tell them you're uncomfortable supporting the players since they don't include your boyfriend."

She chewed her lower lip. "Maybe. That could work."

"And it's Elliot's birthday. You really should be partying with us instead."

Neala pasted a smile on her face. All the excuses that jumped into her mind would mean nothing to Reganne. She was a Crusader now and wanted to support Daniel. If she told Reganne, she'd blow the whole thing out of proportion. Was it really worth it? Couldn't she sneak away for one night and maintain her relationship with The Crusaders and the gang in one place? She squirmed. Why did the thought of lying to both sides make her feel so guilty?

"Hello?" said Reganne. "Earth to Neala! We can expect you to come, right?"

"I have three weeks to decide, Reganne. Don't rush me. Okay?"

Reganne rolled her eyes. "I'll just take that as a yes."

Producing a mock pout, Neala grabbed her pillow under her blanket and threw it at Reganne. Immediately, a brutal pillow fight ensued. As Neala pummeled her friend and avoided blows herself, she tried as hard as she could to forget the trusting blue eyes that had become the best part of her secret life.

CHAPTER 17
DECIDED

Roy crossed his arms. He nodded at Mackenzie. "These records look good, Coach. How much of a chance do you think they have?"

Mackenzie smiled. "Well, the recruiters were very impressed with today's skills review on the field. Based on the speeches that they've been practicing with me, they all might be chosen."

Roy leaned over Mackenzie's desk. "What about the Rookie? I've seen a lot of good things from him at the games."

Mackenzie grinned. "The recruiters are impressed by him the most. If I were to make a wager, I'd say that Daniel is going to be the one. If he gets the scholarship alone, he would probably put Chancellor on the map. Daniel Stevens has big things coming for him."

Roy grinned. This was exactly what his Chancellor needed. The rookie was going to raise the school up high through the glory of the soccer game. It was going to be a victory much bigger than any of Pierce's religious morals. Principal Wilkins straightened to his full height.

"Have the forms for State registration come in yet?"

Coach Mackenzie nodded. "They came in this morning. I'm going to work on them tonight."

"Then I'll leave you to your work."

Roy shut Mackenzie's office door behind him. He paused to run his eyes over the rows of lockers in the locker room. This was his empire. Chancellor would grow to be just what he wanted it to be. He left the locker room, grinning.

†

The ground was hard with winter frost, but that didn't stop two soccer fanatics from blowing off steam in their backyard. Warm in their winter coats and wearing cleats, Art and Daniel kicked the soccer ball to one another. Daniel thought how weird it was to be playing soccer in winter. The lack of snow was another advantage of Georgia. The new cleats his aunt and uncle had given him were firm and smooth beneath him. He caught another pass from Art and began working around his defensive friend.

"So, how did it go with the recruiters today?" Art asked.

"Would you believe flawless?" he replied.

Art laughed. "I would. Bet y'all blew them away."

Daniel shrugged. He passed Art the ball, his angle missing Art by inches.

Art put his hands on his hips. "Now, that is so not what a pass from a future professional should look like."

Shaking his head, he ran past Art to retrieve the ball. With the ball tucked under his arm, he walked back to where his friend stood. He sat down in the grass with a sigh. Art followed.

"Uh-oh. That doesn't sound like someone who is ready for a scholarship. Are you all right?"

Daniel ran a hand over his face. His shoulders slumped. "It's the speech, Art. I...I have it written and Coach Mackenzie approved it, said it was the best one he'd seen, and he couldn't wait to hear it."

Art nodded. He waited for a moment, then replied, "But?"

Daniel shook his head. "It just doesn't feel right. It's almost as if I'm giving all the credit to a jersey with a white letter on the back. The analogy is good but..."

Art nodded. "I see. Well, the speech is supposed to be about something important to you and how you're going to use the scholarship accordingly. It's your chance to show the recruiters what

132

you're all about. If the most important thing for you is a jersey, then talk about your jersey."

Daniel ripped up a blade of grass. He twisted it in his fingers. "And if it's not the most important thing to me?"

"Then find out what is."

Daniel laughed incredulously. "The speech is tomorrow, Art. When am I going to have time to find out what's important to me?"

Art didn't reply. Instead, he stretched his legs out on the lawn and watched the sun go down.

Daniel shot him a crooked grin. "You're going to tell me to pray, aren't you?"

Art smiled. "I was going to tell you to pray, but I figured you already knew the answer to your dilemma." Art glanced down at his wristwatch. "Wow, I've got to get going!" He jumped to his feet. Before heading toward his Jeep, Art looked down at Daniel and winked. "Pray without ceasing, Daniel. God knows you better than you know yourself. Yeah, that's cliché, but it's true. Let Him write His speech for you." Art winked. "See you at Bible study in the morning, Rookie."

Daniel watched his friend go. With a sigh, he lifted himself to his feet and tucked his soccer ball underneath the crook of his arm. He held it close as he walked inside. He had to put the soccer ball away. He had to find some time alone with God and His Word. Then, and only then, would the Holy Spirit tell him what to do. It was time for Daniel to confer with God alone. He left the soccer ball in the hallway, went into his room, and climbed into his closet. The shoes were uncomfortable under him, but he ignored the lumps and bowed his head. In the silence, Daniel prayed.

†

Neala picked up her cell phone. She pushed back her Pre-Calculus book and accepted the call.

"Hello?"

For a moment, the sound of sniffles was all that Neala heard from the other end. She furrowed her brow. "Reganne? Are you okay?"

"Randy broke up with me."

Neala pulled her books against her chest and leaned back in her bungee chair. This didn't make sense. Randy and Reganne were a solid couple since elementary school.

"Why?" she asked.

Reganne blew her nose and cleared her throat. "Now, that is the beautiful part. There was no cheating or drama or argument involved. No, nothing that serious. He…he told me that he's been a Christian for a while and that he is trying to reconnect with God. He said he needs space to find out who God wants him to be and that I'm a distraction. He's one of the freaks, Neala!"

Neala closed her eyes for a second. So, that was why Randy had been at the Crusader Bible Study this morning. Neala had thought he was there to meet Daniel for the morning Conqueror practice. She smiled softly. Leave it to Daniel to find a way through to Randy. Her eyes glanced over at the cover of *Les Misérables* where the Crusader poster hid. What would Reganne think if Neala told her that Randy was not the only one now a part of the "freak" group? She sighed.

"Reganne, I don't think being a Christian necessarily makes Randy a freak. Give him his space. Find out what it is that he is pursuing and maybe then you'll understand."

She snorted. "He's made it very clear that he's pursuing God. He gave me a poster to some Bible study at Art's house. Figures they'd still be running that goon show off campus." She sniffled. "Anyway, I'm not going to the Bible study, and I'm not going to find out Who God is."

Neala bit her lower lip. *Oh, Reganne, I wish I knew how to respond to this. Being a Christian is not so bad.* While Neala gathered thoughts, Reganne cleared her throat again and spoke.

"Hey, forget about Randy for a while. I really need you to come to the party now. It's tomorrow night. Please come, Neala."

Neala ran a hand through her hair. She tapped her pencil against her Pre-Cal book. She had thought of little else for weeks. What could it hurt? She would be with an inconsolable Reganne probably the whole night. Tomorrow morning she could break the news to Daniel, give him some excuse during Bible study as to why she wasn't going to come hear his scholarship speech. Neala sighed.

"I'll be there."

†

Daniel pushed the print button and then leaned back. The sound of the printer feeding and releasing pages of his speech confirmed his final decision. The work was only half done. Once the pages were printed, Daniel picked them up and read over his notes. His heartbeat quickened. Images of the Bible study mixed with hours spent on the field filled his mind. Yes, it was all sorted. The rookie knew what was important to him. Thanks to hours spent in prayer, Daniel knew what he had to say.

CHAPTER 18
TONIGHT

Daniel inhaled and exhaled repeatedly. The crowd was filing in; he could hear them mingling with each other from behind the gym stage. The curtain did little to lessen his nerves. He pulled on his sports coat, straightened the stiff, white collar underneath, and made sure that all of the components of his speech were in place. He glanced over at Randy and Hank. Hank paced back and forth, keeping his attention on his notes instead of his competitors. He was in his own arena tonight.

Randy settled next to Daniel. He took a deep breath and winked. "Did you get a prayer note today? Hank and I both found one on top of our speech notes. I really don't know how this anonymous prayer person does it, but it's really kind of awesome. You know, to think that God has someone out there praying for us."

Daniel nodded. He pulled on his red tie. "Yes," he agreed, "it's awesome."

From the stage, Principal Wilkins began addressing the crowd to open the assembly. Hank scurried back to his seat. Randy gripped Daniel on the shoulder.

"Remember," he whispered, "we're not in this alone. Right, Daniel?"

Daniel smiled and nodded. That thought stayed with him as the curtains opened to reveal a gym full of guests. The recruiters sat near the front and each Crusader had promised to attend. Well, all but one. Neala had given no explanation as to her absence. Daniel forced himself to forget about her and focus on his mission for tonight. Tonight was a night for change.

Hank stood to open the round of speeches from the three contestants. Daniel took a deep breath. He trained hard to reach this point. His work would pay off tonight. He didn't fear what he had to say. He knew the words he needed to speak when he took the stage. This was God's night.

†

Neala stood on the steps of Reganne's porch. The cool night air brushed against her bare arms, making her shiver. She watched the lights and shadows converging behind closed blinds. Laughter spilled from the house with the beat of boisterous music. The noises called to her, inviting her into the gaiety of the life she'd always known. Yet, her heart seemed to tug at her, weighing her down and nailing her to the bottom step.

Don't do this. Turn around.

Neala rolled her eyes, pushing her hair out of her face. "What is wrong with you?" she whispered. "You've been going to Reganne's parties all your life."

But that was before Daniel. She took a deep breath, looking over her shoulder. It wasn't too late to back out. She could fake an illness on Reganne just as she had her Mom and Roy. She could go back home and hide from everyone. She'd still be lying to both sides but…

The front door swung open. "Neala!"

Neala turned around, an insincere smile immediately falling over her face. Wow, she hadn't realized how quickly she could pin on her mask. Reganne hurried down the stairs, throwing her arms around her.

"I thought you'd never get here!"

She laughed nervously. "Well, I did have to wait for Mom and Roy to leave."

138

Reganne squeezed her shoulders, making her way up the stairs with Neala in tow. "It doesn't matter, you're here now. Come on, the whole gang is here, and the party is underway. Best night ever!"

Elliot met them at the door. In the space of a second, when Reganne let go and Elliot reached for her, Neala thought about running. But then Elliot's hands closed around hers. It was too late. She took a deep breath, crossing the threshold into the party. Her stomach flip-flopped. *I'll be fine. I can handle this. No problem at all.* She gripped the strap of her purse as the door closed behind her. It was the least she could hope for.

†

The applause died down as Randy took his place next to Daniel. His speech had been perfect, his oration flawless, his points executed. Daniel took a deep breath. Now, it was his turn. Randy winked at him as he was called. He gathered his jersey in his hands and moved to the center of the stage.

The bright lights cast the audience in shadows, but he could hear the number of people in the crowd, shifting, waiting. In the front, the recruiters would be taking notes. Daniel placed his own notes on top of the podium, waiting for the applause to stop. He cleared his throat. His hands trembled. Today, the season came to a peak. Today, the important things were at hand. He closed his eyes for a second. Then, Daniel spoke.

"From the first game I played this soccer season, I earned the name, the Rookie. Even now, as I am standing here trying to reach for the ultimate scholarship, the Rookie is a name that has stuck with me." He paused and cleared his throat. He held up his jersey for all to see. "I was initially going to talk about my jersey tonight. I was going to talk about how number nine has carried me through the tough times of the season and has helped me reach this point. Last night, however, when reviewing my speech, I realized that everything I was going to talk about was wrong. I realized that I had gained the right to stand on this stage through another source. So, tonight, I would like to talk about my Father."

Daniel heard someone turning pages below him. His scholarship form showed both of his parents as deceased. He laid his jersey across the podium. "My adoptive Father."

The pages stopped turning. Every movement in the assembly ceased.

"When I was only five years old, I lost my biological father to tuberculosis. Most would define that as tragic, and in many ways it was. But I was never alone because my mother introduced me to my adoptive Father the night that my biological father died. We were awkward with each other at first, but He never left my side. He played with me in the shadows of childhood and helped me chase the Sonshine. Then, one happy day when I was eight years old, He gave me His name in the small room of a white wooden building. Before officially becoming my Father, however, He gave me a gift. The gift was enclosed in a white box with red ribbon. He opened the box for me, showing me what He had prepared for me years before we had even met. It was a gift He had begun to craft when He created the world."

Daniel paused here to hold up a box like the one he had described. His hands still trembling, he lifted the top of the box and laid both the top and main part of the box to the side. He placed his hand inside and pulled out five swaths of material. He draped the first one over the center of the podium. The black swath looked ominous against the lighted stage.

"My adoptive Father told me that, before I became His son, I had to realize a very important thing. I had to realize that, as a human, I was a sinner. He told me sin had made my heart black and that for that reason I could never be his Son. In His book, the Bible, my Father wrote, "As it is written, There is none righteous, no, not one." And He also wrote "For all have sinned, and come short of the glory of God." After I told Him that I understood this, He told me that I had to pay a price for being a sinner and that price was death and Hell. Hell was a horrible place where fire would consume me forever. 'For the wages of sin is death…'." As a little eight-year-old boy, I understood that I had a dark heart, and I definitely did not want to go to Hell. I also

140

understood I could not go to Heaven on my own." Daniel paused and unfolded a red swath of cloth. He draped it next to the black one.

"Then, my Father began opening the best part of the gift. He told me that, in order to make it possible for me to become His son, He had given up His only Son Jesus Christ and had allowed Him to shed His blood to make my heart white and clean. His Son did so when He hung on a cross called Calvary at a hill called Golgotha" Daniel placed a white cloth on the other side of the black one. "For God so loved the world, that he gave his only begotten Son, that whosoever believeth in him should not perish but have everlasting life." Daniel added a yellow cloth next to the white one. "Eternal life in Heaven was another part of my Father's gift. Three days after His Son's death, my Father gave His Son victory over death, and Jesus rose from the grave. Then, after ministering to others, His Son Jesus went to Heaven, a place of gold and rest, to prepare a place for all those that believed on Him. He is still there today."

From the back of the gym, Daniel heard a string of curses burst forth. The back door opened and a few people left the room. The recruiters hadn't moved since he took out his first cloth. People were shifting in their seats and whispering to each other. He caught sight of the jersey. He turned away from it and pulled out his final piece of cloth. The emerald green swatch shimmered as he placed it beside the white one.

"If I believed in my adoptive Father's Word, He also promised me that He would help me grow in Him daily and that He would send me His Spirit to watch over me. After He presented His gift to me, I gladly took on His name and became a Christian by simply kneeling by myself in that little room and praying for Him to give me that gift. That day, I officially became His son. When I took on His name, I promised that I would tell other dark or orphaned hearts about Him, and I would live as a mirror of Him because His gift was for the whole world, not just me."

Daniel took a deep breath. He looked down at the audience. "Through this love and sacrifice that my adoptive Father gave to me when I was eight years old, I have come to this spot in my life. Through examples of His Word, the Bible, I have formed the ethics that have led me to great heights in my passion for soccer. Every time I run onto the field, I play for Him, not the coach or the fans. That is why I want this scholarship. More than anything, I want to share this gift that my adoptive Father gave me with others. I want to help others come to know His grace and mercy. I want to begin a redemption program someday using soccer to bring other young men and women to Christ. God is the greatest Coach I could have ever asked for, and He never leaves. He is at every game I play in as He is here with me now. I hope you will consider me for the scholarship. Thank you."

As Daniel gathered his illustrations, no one applauded. The gym was so quiet that Daniel wondered if perhaps the whole audience had gotten up and walked out. He walked back to his seat. Randy reached over and shook his hand. Then, with a wink, he began applauding. His applause was the only sound for several minutes. Then another clap answered his. Soon, the whole gym was clapping. They were not as enthusiastic as they had been for the previous speeches, but at least Daniel could tell they were present.

Principal Wilkins stepped forward to conclude the assembly. As the gym began to empty and Wilkins went to meet with the recruiters, Daniel stayed glued to his spot on the stage. The hostile gazes he received from many of the adults and most of the students sent waves of dread over him. He thought of the party Art had prepared to celebrate his triumphant victory tonight. He glanced down at his jersey. He knew one thing for certain. He'd just given up the scholarship, but His Father was proud. More than ever before, tonight, Daniel was God's soccer player.

Daniel stood and walked off the gym stage. He found his guardians to inform them that he was going to walk to Art's house for the party. Although they were hesitant to leave him, they finally conceded. Daniel waited until he saw them drive off. Then, he began to run. He wasn't sure where he was going, but he was getting as far away as possible from the culmination of his life's dream and the hard eyes of the world.

CHAPTER 19
SEEN

Daniel slowed his jog to a walk. Despite the cool night, sweat beaded his brow and drenched his body. His heart pounded in his chest as he tried to bring his breathing back to normal. He wiped sweat from his eyes. How long had he run? An hour? Two?

He paused to catch his breath, noticing the shadows cast by the huge houses in the neighborhood where he now stood. He started walking slowly down the sidewalk. His damp dress shirt made him itch, and the surroundings of the high-class suburbs reminded him that he didn't belong. He stuffed his hands into his pockets.

Now what, God? What am I supposed to do?

Daniel sighed. It would be easier to resent this turn of events if a sense of peace were not so intertwined with his confusion. Would he ever get another opportunity like this scholarship? He'd done the right thing, but it still didn't make sense.

He paused before a driveway full of cars. Music blasted from inside to where he stood. A few of the cars had Chancellor High bumper stickers on them. Students stood on the steps of the house, smoking and laughing. Daniel took a deep breath. Is this really what everyone wanted from life?

He turned as a group of teens burst from the house, laughing and clinging to each other. Disgust filled him. His shoulders slumped. What could he do to help others against so many temptations? At least he could depend on The Crusaders to always do what's right.

As he began walking down the sidewalk, the voices of the teens rose, carrying to where he stood.

"Seriously guys, I'm done. I need to get home."

"Come on, Girl! The night just started."

Daniel narrowed his eyes. Even as blurred as it sounded, he knew that first voice. Neala? Why was she here? He turned slightly, looking over his shoulder. The group had stopped in front of a truck and were passing around drinks. He recognized the vehicle right away. In the dim light, he could see Neala trying to pull away from arms that held her too close. Anger coursed through him. Elliot! He wasn't going to let the bully mess with one of his Crusaders. Dropping his gym bag, he stomped toward the pickup truck.

"Please, Elliot," begged Neala, "just let me go."

Elliot laughed, ignoring her request and leaning against the hood of the vehicle, dragging her with him.

"Hey!" Daniel shouted. All eyes of the group turned to him. He clenched his fists. "Let her go, Elliot."

Elliot straightened, his arms never leaving Neala's waist. She shook her head, eyes wide as he stopped before them. Daniel ignored Neala's warning. "I'm not asking you again."

The other teens around them slowly backed away. A few snickered, turning toward the house and whispering to each other. Only one other girl stayed behind. Reganne glanced between Daniel and Elliot.

"Okay, guys, let's cool it," said Reganne. "I promised the parents I'd keep the cops away from this one."

Daniel kept his eyes fixed on Elliot. "I'm keeping my cool. Just waiting for Elliot to be a gentleman and let Neala go."

Elliot shrugged. "Neala doesn't deserve a gentleman."

At those words, all the frustrations of the day overflowed. Heaving a deep breath, he lunged at Elliot, bringing his fist to meet the center of his face. Fire swept across his knuckles as Elliot groaned, releasing Neala and falling to the ground. Daniel braced himself for further confrontation. One blow was all it took. Reganne yelped, bending down to push Elliot over. Despite a bruise forming on his nose, he remained unhurt. Daniel grimaced.

Reganne jumped back to her feet, arms crossed, glaring at Daniel. "You better hope he doesn't try to press charges! Now leave. You weren't invited."

Daniel glanced over at Neala. She stood where Elliot had left her, head hanging low and cheeks bright red. He frowned. Blood pounding through his head, he turned and left both girls in the cold. Reganne took a few minutes to rant at Neala. The sound of the door shutting ended the conversation. Soft sobs rose on the wind. *Neala.*

He frowned, taking the last few steps to the sidewalk while flexing his throbbing fist. Let her find her own way home. He'd done enough for her. It was time for her to see what it felt like to be abandoned. *I'm done helping those who don't want help! I'm not responsible for her!*

He winced, slowing down as his heart twisted within him. He glanced down at the palm of his fist. This very same palm had caught her tears just a few months back. If he left her now, how could he claim to be any better than Elliot? She didn't need judgement right now. She needed a true friend.

He sighed. Taking a deep breath, he turned and approached her again. She leaned against Elliot's truck, covering her face with her hands and shivering against the coolness of the night. He slipped his sports coat off his shoulders, holding it out to her and clearing his throat.

Neala looked up, eyes wide as she glanced between the coat and Daniel. With trembling fingers, she took the coat, throwing it over her bare shoulders.

Daniel placed his hands in his pant pockets. "Come on, I'll walk you home," he whispered.

Neala shook her head. "I don't think..."

"We don't have to talk but it's getting dark out. I just want to make sure you get there safely."

There was a moment of silence. Would she deny him again? Then she pulled away from the truck, whispering a simple: "Okay."

Daniel took the lead, walking down the sidewalk with Neala following beside him. They both walked quietly into the crisp fall night.

†

You should have left me by the truck.

Neala scrunched her shoulders deeper into Daniel's sports coat. At least he had kept talking to a minimum. She kept her eyes on her feet. Why, of all people, did he have to be the one to show up? Her emotions crashed inside her, filling her with guilt and dread all the way home. The walk seemed twice as long. For the first time in her life, she felt relieved when she approached the door to her apartment. Daniel kept an even pace, walking her to the front door and stopping in the light of the entry way. She groaned inwardly, closing her eyes. *Okay. You saved the day. Just let me go and don't say anything else.*

For a moment, she thought he might have heard her thoughts. Then, his strong calming voice cut the silence hanging between them.

"Are you okay now?"

Neala's eyes flew open. No questions about her betrayal? No accusations about why she abandoned him? Her guilt spilled over into frustration, the question chafing at her nerves. Shrugging off his sports jacket, she shoved it toward him. "You're always asking me that! Are you okay? Can I help you? Well, I'm not okay and you can't help me, so stop trying." She stepped closer, ignoring the irrational tone of her own voice. "Just look at me Daniel. LOOK AT ME!"

Daniel winced. She hung her head, stepping back as her anger gathered in the form of nausea at the base of her stomach. She felt tears coming again. Couldn't she ever do anything right?

"I see you," said Daniel.

She shook her head. "Do you? Do you really?"

Daniel paused for a moment. Then he nodded slowly. "Yes. I see a girl broken by human hands that can't be mended by human hands. I see a girl fighting so hard to fit into a world that cares nothing about her. I see a broken soul, begging for healing yet refusing the only thing that can make it whole. I see a beautiful person who is letting

146

the world destroy her future." He slipped his coat over his dress shirt. "You're right about one thing. I can't help you. But you know Who can. Neither of us is going to force you. You must accept the help. It's your choice, Neala."

She shook her head, squeezing her eyes shut as new tears rolled down her cheeks. Elliot's words echoed in her mind. Daniel hadn't seen her yet, not really. He would walk out of her life just like everyone else.

"Neala, look at me."

His warm gentle voice seemed to move her chin upward. Elliot's taunts diminished. She opened her eyes to find him watching her, calmly and patiently, not an ounce of malice or disgust marring his blue eyes. No one had ever looked at her like this. It was pure, undefiled, unrelenting love. She gasped at the thought.

"Neala," he whispered. "I wish I could decide this for you, but I can't. I wish I could be the one to pull you out of all that's dragging you down. The one thing I can do is never stop praying for you. You'll get beyond this. And I promise, even if you don't believe me, I'm not walking away from you."

She looked into his honest blue eyes. She balled her hands into fists. "Daniel," she said. "Why are you so…"

Daniel held up his hand, stopping her words. "I'm not," he said.

Offering her one last smile, he said a gentle good night and walked away. Neala wrapped her arms around herself as she watched him go. The wind breached the space he'd emptied, whispering unspoken words into her ear. *God is.*

She rubbed her arms as the shadows swallowed up Daniel. Every piece of her wanted to believe him. She wanted to believe he'd stay constant. She glanced up to the sky. *I want to believe You care like he does God.* Clouds covered the small sliver of moonlight breaking through the darkness. With a sigh, she bent down, found the hidden key under the doormat, and fumbled with the lock of the front door.

The house was dark and silent. No one had checked in on her. No one was waiting nervously for her to arrive home. Jane had forgotten about her again. Noiselessly, she shut the door behind her. Her hands searched for the smooth white wall to her left, using it as a guide to her room. When she found the second door in the hallway, she slipped into the cocoon of her room and shut the world behind her. Here she was again. Alone.

She slid to the floor, too tired to find her way to her bed. Sobs rose and escaped again. Would she ever stop crying? She hit the floor over and over again. Daniel's words washed over her, fighting against her fears. She wanted so much to escape the world she knew. But what if she found herself in a new life just as dark and dismal as the one she had now? She curled up on the floor, shivering as exhaustion overtook her. As sleep claimed her, fear won over her hope. That love she thought she saw in Daniel's eyes was just her imagination. She didn't deserve to be loved. Just as always before, that kind of love was just the remnant of dreams.

CHAPTER 20
CHARACTER

"Neala!"

Neala groaned. She turned to find Elliot running toward her. Without a second glance, she kept walking toward Chancellor High, quickening her pace. For three days, she'd ignored every phone call and text from the gang. She'd purposely dragged her feet this morning so she could get to school just in time to avoid their morning gossip ring. She trembled as she heard Elliot getting closer. Just a few more feet...

Elliot's hand gripped her shoulder, stopping her at the bottom of the entrance steps. "Neala. I called you. Didn't you hear me?"

She cleared her throat, pulling her shoulder away and turning toward him. "Yeah, um, sorry. Running a little late today."

She turned back toward the steps, but Elliot jumped in front of her. He crossed his arms, smirking. "Whoa there. Not so fast. Jeez, it's like you're trying to avoid me or something."

She noticed the dark bruise around his nose for the first time. It took all her willpower not to smirk back. His bravado only made the bruise more noticeable. She sighed. "Well, maybe I am."

He rolled his eyes. "Come on. You're not still mad about the party! So, I said a few things I shouldn't have. I was just trying to get the saintly Daniel to move on."

Neala frowned. "It's not just what you said, it's what you did."

"What did I do?"

"Exactly! You did nothing! You didn't listen to me or respect my wishes. I'm not yours to control, Elliot."

Elliot chuckled. He jumped down beside her and threw his arms around her shoulders. "It's never bothered you before."

Neala's head throbbed, every sense on edge at his closeness. With one firm shove, she broke his hold on her shoulders. "That's it! I'm done with you. Do you hear me? I'm done being a fool. Leave me alone, okay!"

She didn't wait for his response. As the school bell rang across campus, she began running up the stairs.

Elliot called after her. "Maybe you prefer that religious freak. Don't be stupid, Neala. He's about to lose everything."

Neala pushed her way through the crowd at the front door and ran into Chancellor High. Students milled around her, oblivious to the sobs fighting their way through her system. She took deep breaths, leaning against a row of lockers. Daniel was about to lose everything? She didn't even want to know what that meant.

As Reganne passed, Neala held her breath. She didn't want to face her either. Where had she been the night when Elliot had almost forced himself on her? Where had her mother been that night when Neala wanted her hugs and reassurance? Only one person had been brave enough to reach out to her. She bit her trembling lower lip. Had he prayed for her when she didn't show up to Bible study this morning? The thought was more than she could bear.

A group of laughing students caught Neala's attention. Shifting her backpack, she leaned over and peeked beyond the shadows. Her eyes narrowed. There was a group of students surrounding Daniel's locker. She moved closer, shoving her way through the crowd until she saw what had their attention.

Her eyes widened. She forgot her headache when she caught sight of their morning entertainment. Daniel stood in front of his locker, hands formed into fists, face red as he faced the object that had brought about the laughter. A graffiti image of a torn Bible and one horrifying word were etched on the face of Daniel's locker. It was the worst imaginable word for an orphan.

Neala covered her mouth and squeezed her eyes shut. How dare they do this? Wasn't he the Rookie, big soccer hero, about to win a scholarship? Dare they mess with him like that?

"Serves him right," whispered one of Neala's classmates standing next to her, "after what he did at the scholarship ceremony."

Neala gave her classmate a sideways glance. *The ceremony?* She watched Daniel approach his locker. He opened it and reached for his books, trying to ignore the crowd and go on as usual. This time, however, Neala noticed that his hands trembled when his fingers brushed up against the graffiti. She turned to escape the scene as Elliot walked through Chancellor's front doors. He crossed his arms and grinned. Neala shook her head, running to the bathroom as fast as she could.

When she closed the stall door, the sobs came. None of this should be happening. Wasn't God watching over Daniel? She heard the first hour bell ring but ignored it. She leaned against the stall door. For the first time in her life, she wished she knew how she could help an orphan's heart mend.

†

"Stevens! Come into my office."

Daniel looked up from securing his cleats. Mackenzie stood in the doorway of his office with a folder in his hands. Behind him, Daniel could see Principal Wilkins waiting. Randy caught Daniel's eyes. He nodded, slung his gym bag over his shoulder, and slapped Daniel on the back. His eyes told him that Randy would be praying as his friend faced whatever was waiting for him with the coach. Hank scurried past Daniel sending him an awkward glance of pity.

Daniel took a deep breath. He grabbed his own gym bag and walked over to Mackenzie's office. His thighs burned from the day's practice, and his mind burned from all of the invectives that had been thrown at him throughout the day. He entered the coach's office and closed the door behind him. His heart pumping in his chest, he faced both Coach Mackenzie and Principal Wilkins.

Principal Wilkins crossed his arms over his chest. "Take a seat, Rookie."

Daniel settled in one of the chairs behind him.

Principal Wilkins shook his head. "I'll get right to the point, Stevens. Your speech at the scholarship ceremony was unacceptable. I don't want anyone to get the wrong impression about our school. The recruiters were confused and a few horrified." He paused and glanced at Mackenzie. "However, they were impressed by your skills on the field." He leaned across Mackenzie's desk. "Son, we're willing to offer you another chance."

Daniel's eyes widened. Another chance at his dream? He stopped when he saw the cold eyes of the principal. What was the cost? As if reading his thoughts, Principal Wilkins continued.

"The recruiters want to set up a private session in which you will give them another speech, void of religious sentiment, and show them that you are serious about playing professional soccer. They don't want to hear about your faith; they want to hear about your secular intentions for the scholarship."

Daniel swallowed hard. "With all due respect, I have no secular intentions for the scholarship."

"This is not a game, Daniel. Show me enough character to conform to my regulations."

Daniel glanced down at the jersey in his hands. No, this wasn't a game. Soccer was a game, but this decision wasn't. His fingers played with the silk jersey. Marks of dirt, grass stains, and a small tear in the upper left corner testified to the struggles he'd pushed through to get this close to his dream. Daniel licked his lips and looked between Principal Wilkins and Coach Mackenzie.

"Character," he whispered. Daniel stood to his feet and placed his gym bag over his shoulder. He looked calmly into Principal Wilkins' eyes. "If it's character you're looking for Principal Wilkins, it's character I'll give you." He turned to Coach Mackenzie. "I would like to withdraw from the team." He placed his jersey across the desk.

Coach Mackenzie's eyes widened. "Daniel, think about all that you're giving up."

Principal Wilkins frowned. "Is your God worth all of this, Daniel?"

He looked at his number nine jersey. More than anything in the world he wanted that jersey back in his hands. Instead, he answered Principal Wilkins. "Yes, Sir. He is."

Both men sat in silence as Daniel turned and exited the office. He walked through the locker room in a daze. It wasn't until he stepped into the cold winter air and began walking across the parking lot that he realized what he'd done. At the ceremony, he'd thought that his dreams were coming to an end. Now, they truly had.

Daniel paused in the middle of the parking lot. He closed his eyes, stuffing his hands into his pockets. The breeze ripped around him, biting, biting, ever biting just as the people around him had been throughout the entire day. Would it ever end? He took deep breaths and tried to find peace. *God, help me understand. God, please help me.*

Something nudged Daniel painfully in the side. His eyes flew open as a shadow fell over him. He felt a spirit of oppression even before he turned to the recipients of that shadow. When he caught sight of Elliot and two of his companions standing mere inches away from him, his whole body tensed. Elliot held his backpack. Daniel swallowed hard.

Not now.

Elliot's sneer accentuated the bruise Daniel had given him a few nights earlier. He opened the flap of Daniel's backpack and stuffed his hands into its contents.

Daniel straightened and took a step forward. "Can I help you with something?"

Elliot dropped Daniel's backpack to the ground, and his hands emerged holding Daniel's Bible.

"Nah," he said, "I found what I was looking for. This Bible. It's supposedly indestructible. Your Father's Book, right? His promises?"

Daniel watched warily as Elliot opened the Bible with exaggerated carefulness. "So, how important is Your Father to you again?"

153

Daniel ached to touch the Bible. He needed God to speak to him. "He's everything..."

The sound of tearing pages cut off his reply. He watched with wide eyes as pages from his Bible fluttered out of Elliot's hands and into the wind. The pages were followed by peals of laughter. As Elliot's hands gripped the edge of his Bible again, anger boiled up inside of Daniel. He lunged forward; his hand opened in order to reclaim his lifeline. Just as his fingers touched the outer edge of the Bible, Elliot's two companions grabbed his wrists and jerked him backward.

Elliot scattered more of God's Word on the ground. Daniel elbowed Elliot's two friends, and they released him to catch their breaths. He took the chance and moved toward Elliot again. Without looking up, Elliot drove his knee into Daniel's gut. He gasped but refused to double over. They could not have his Bible.

Elliot looked up, tossed the Bible on the hood of the nearest car, and cracked his knuckles. He blocked Daniel's next blow and delivered a punch to Daniel's stomach. Daniel groaned, pressed his ribcage with one hand, and repositioned his fist with another. As his fist rose, it was captured again and his arms twisted painfully behind him. Elliot's friends had Daniel in their hands again.

The next few minutes became a matter of taking one painful breath at a time. Elliot pummeled Daniel with jabs and uppercuts, taking obvious pleasure in his brutal attack. When he finally stepped back and Elliot's friends released him, Daniel's bruised body collapsed. He slumped to the ground, his body quivering and blood filling his mouth. Elliot moved to kick Daniel in the ribs, but he paused when he heard the sound of footsteps coming across the parking lot. He spat on the cement next to Daniel's face. Then, dropping the Bible next to him, the three of them left him at the mercy of whoever was approaching and ran across the parking lot, ducking between cars.

Daniel stared at the tattered remnants of his Bible. The wind picked up, and Daniel knew more of his treasured pages were being scattered across the parking lot. Still, he did not, could not, move. His body pulsed with pain. Every breath he took cut like a sharp knife. He closed his eyes and groaned as the footsteps drew closer. This is not how it's supposed to be. The footsteps stopped and gentle fingertips brushed against one of his bruises. A familiar voice called out to him and he winced. Humiliation was the worst part of the pain.

CHAPTER 21
BROKEN

Neala saw him lying on the ground. Before she could wonder what happened, she was rushing to his side. She'd never seen Daniel looking so helpless. As she neared him, her eyes skimmed the parking lot. Who would dare attack him like this? A name popped into her mind, and she shook her head. *One thing at a time.*

She stopped beside him, dropped her piano books, and fell to her knees. His eyes were closed, but she could see pain wrinkling his features. She put a finger against his temple, grazing one of the bruises that had begun to form. Trembling and biting her lower lip, she gently shook his shoulders.

"Daniel? Daniel, can you hear me? Are you okay? Daniel!"

His eyes flew open. "That is sooo not helping my headache, Neala."

Neala was relieved to hear the normal, though slightly strained tone of his voice. "What happened? Who did this?"

He shook his head. "It was a long time coming." He tried to lift himself up but instead fell back and closed his eyes. "Is there any way I can get a ride home?"

Neala nodded. Her mother would just have to wait for the car a little longer this afternoon. She led Daniel to the passenger's side of her car and helped him get in. He fell against the leather seat with an "oomph." His head rested on the headrest out of sheer need. After helping him maneuver the seatbelt to lessen pressure around his ribs, she shut the passenger door.

As Neala rounded the corner to approach the driver's door, her foot tripped over the leather binding of Daniel's Bible. She bent to pick up the remains. The wind caressed the tattered pages. Her eyes caught sight of dutiful and passionate notes in the margin, highlighted verses, and outlines of sermons. The binding was not as full as it was made to be, but it continued to be a testament to its owner.

She glanced at the nebulous clouds above her. Had he fought for this Bible? Was it really worth all this trouble? What was it about God that made Daniel willing to suffer to such an extent? She knew a lot of facts about God and the Bible, but what was it that made Daniel the way he was? She picked up a few of the Bible pages that she could find, placed them back into the binding, and climbed into the car. Before turning on the ignition, she placed the Bible on Daniel's lap. He covered it with his swollen fingers, eyes still closed, and nodded slightly. The ride home was silent.

†

All Daniel could think of was his physical pain. As Neala helped him to the door of his house, he marveled at the irony of the situation. Only days earlier, he'd been the one helping her to the door. He leaned against the stone wall behind them, smiling at God's sense of humor.

After a few knocks, Aunt Lisa opened the door. Her eyes captured Daniel, supported by a stone wall with his Bible against his heaving ribs. She rushed him into the house, asking Neala a flurry of questions and settling him on the couch in the living room. Neala filled her in on what she knew about the situation. For the next few minutes, Aunt Lisa was a whirlwind. Incessantly asking questions about his pains, she moved from the kitchen to the living room and sent Neala from one closet to another to get supplies. Finally, all of Daniel's minor bleeding had stopped and his major abrasions were bandaged or iced.

Aunt Lisa settled in a loveseat next to the couch Daniel lay on. Her body was stiff and rigid as she took a deep breath. "Did you fight back?" she whispered.

He nodded. "Sure I did, but I had only two fists. They had six." He made an attempt at a smile.

Aunt Lisa picked up the Bible that sat on Daniel's knee. She leafed through the tattered pages. Finally, she sighed and slapped both covers shut between her hands. She gave him a hard look. "Are you done?"

Daniel knit his brow. "Done?"

Aunt Lisa shook her head. "This has gone too far. I think you made your point at the scholarship ceremony."

He straightened. "I fought for God today. Are you asking me to quit?"

She closed her eyes, gathering her thoughts. "Look, Daniel, I'm very proud of who you are and what you've been doing at school. However, there is a point when it is time to bow out. Be an example, but the world can only take so much Christian zeal at a time. Daniel, have your Bible study, stay involved in church, but take a step back. Moderation, Daniel; show them in moderation."

For a few moments, Daniel just stared at Aunt Lisa. Then, he hung his head and slumped his shoulders. Pushing on the edge of the couch to gain momentum, he got to his feet. Neala came forward to help him, but he shook his head. Without another word, he moved down the hall and into his room.

Daniel shut the door behind him. He heard the rise and fall of voices from the living room, and then, after the slamming of the front door, he was surrounded by silence. Once again, he was alone.

He placed his tattered Bible on the edge of his bed. As he lowered his weight onto the other side, the Bible teetered and fell off balance. Instantly, the torn pieces of Scripture Neala saved from the parking lot covered the floor. God's promises from the prophets and His Son stared up at Daniel, their edges frayed. He closed his eyes and lowered himself to the floor. With all the vehemence he could muster, he pummeled his mattress. Why should he keep doing this?

Why should he pray for a world that so blatantly threw God's promises to the side? Tears of anger and frustration poured down his face.

"Am I alone?" he cried out.

Sobs shook his shoulders. All the weight that he'd been carrying pressed in on him and he let the burdens wash over him. He wiped his face and gazed at the ceiling.

"Have You forsaken me, God? Why aren't You here with me? Where are Your blessings? I've done everything You've told me to do! I gave You the scholarship, my popularity as a soccer player, all my dreams, and respect from the student body. I laid it all at Your feet. Where are You? Do You want me to quit? I don't understand."

His mother's words slipped into his mind. "It's all right to fight with God sometimes…it just makes you realize how right He was all along."

Daniel crawled into bed. His bones ached with every move he made. He closed his eyes. He refused to fight any longer. If the world didn't want God, he would keep Him to himself. He reached for sleep; but throughout the night, he continued to wrestle with God.

✝

Neala stepped outside with Aunt Lisa trailing behind her. She stood silently next to Daniel's aunt.

Aunt Lisa sniffled and wiped her face with the back of her hand. "Thank you so much for bringing him home," she said. "I'm sorry you had to see all of this. That boy! Both of his parents were so sensible, but I just don't know what has gotten into him."

Neala gazed up at the moon through the treetops. "He calls it faith."

Aunt Lisa snorted. "There is a difference between faith and foolishness. He needs to be more discreet."

Neala cocked her head. Something about those words didn't seem quite right for the bruised and battered guy inside this house. Did faith have to be calculated and logical?

"You have heard of WWJD, haven't you?" she asked.

"Of course I have."

Neala fished the car keys out of her pocket. "I think that's what Daniel's doing. I don't know much about faith, but I do know that it has been a long time since I've seen God in someone. Why do Christians have to be discreet?" Neala swallowed hard. "Good night, Mrs. Stevens."

Neala didn't look back at the speechless woman she left in the doorway. As she pressed her keys into the ignition, she mulled over the words she had just spoken. She actually believed them. Daniel really was the spitting image of Jesus, especially today, beaten for his faith and scorned by his family. Perhaps this cost was why she just couldn't fully trust God. Was she ready to give up everything for Him?"

For God so loved the world...

Neala parked her car. She took a deep breath. Did love abandon so easily? Was Daniel alone in all of this? She gazed up at the sky. Somewhere, past the neon lights, there were stars. According to the Bible, past all of those stars was God. Neala thought again of Daniel's bruises. Why did love hurt so much?

Tentatively, she closed her eyes. For a second, she wasn't sure what to do next. She began to whisper.

"God, it's Neala. I'm not sure You really care about much of what I say, but You listen to every word spoken on earth, I guess. So, please help Daniel." Neala paused, at a loss for words. How did one talk to God? "Help him...just help him."

A tear trickled down her cheek. She kept her eyes closed and trembled in the darkness. Yes, this kind of love hurt. She wrapped her arms around herself and began to wonder if prayer ever made Daniel cry.

CHAPTER 22
DREAMS

Daniel wiped his brow. Even on this dark cloudy morning, his daily jog had him soaked in sweat. He rolled his eyes. Why wasn't this getting easier? This was the third day he had gone out on his own and every moment seemed to get more frustrating. Maybe he should have called Art. Daniel frowned at the thought. No, the last thing he needed was more questions.

As he rounded the last corner of Chancellor High, he noticed the gate that closed off the soccer field was swinging back and forth. The squeak of its hinges stopped him in his tracks. He paused next to the gate, his breath shallow from exertion. The green field called to him as it had the first time he saw it. He looked from left to right to make sure no one was watching. Then, he slipped onto the field. It was eerie to walk across the field before the sun rose. The fog that clung to the ground made him shiver as it enveloped him in wisps.

He rested on a spot on the lower bleachers, his running shoes planted firmly on the ground he had torn up with cleats during the fall. He looked at the green expanse. It looked so empty. Surely in his mind he could fill it up with fans again. He squinted. Frowning, he yanked a few blades of grass from the ground. If only he had the scholarship. Daniel allowed the wind to scatter the blades of grass in his open palm until one blade was left. He closed a fist around that blade of grass. What did he have left?

"So, you finally came to join me."

He turned from his thoughts toward the voice behind him. He was surprised when he saw Mr. Pierce coming from behind the bleachers and approaching him. He smiled kindly at Daniel.

"May I share this bleacher?"

Daniel hesitated. Then, he conceded and returned his gaze to the field.

The bleachers creaked as he sat with a sigh. "This is a good place to sit and think."

Daniel nodded silently. The skies were starting to grow light with the oncoming morning, but no sign of sunshine licked the sky yet.

"It's also a good place to share them with somebody. Care to share your thoughts?" asked Mr. Pierce.

"Not really."

"Well, I'd like to share mine, if you're willing to listen."

Daniel shrugged. This was just what he needed…an old man reminiscing about his life.

Mr. Pierce pointed toward the rear view of Chancellor's building which faced the soccer field. "What do you think of Chancellor High?"

Daniel emitted a bitter laugh before he could stop it. The intense emotions that responded to that question overwhelmed him. He cast a sideways glance at Mr. Pierce.

A sad smile lifted the corners of his lips. "I've felt the same way for so long." He cocked his head. "Have you ever wondered why the school is so close to Trinity?"

Daniel glanced across the walkway that separated the church and school. He furrowed his brow. What was the big deal?

Mr. Pierce sighed. "You know, Daniel, Chancellor High wasn't always a government-owned facility. When I was your age, Trinity and Chancellor were one and the same. Granted, the facilities were much smaller."

Daniel cleared his throat. Should he take notes? He shifted. Mr. Pierce pointed to the field.

"I used to play here too. I was the team's goalkeeper. Trinity's preacher at the time was my father, and he had big plans for the school. Little by little, however, his big plans allowed things to creep into the school. From my freshman year to my senior year, I noticed immorality, incorrect doctrine, and immovable apathy creeping through the student body. Then, one of our students brought a financial suit against the school during my senior year. Everyone was a bit shaken, but we assumed God would do His thing. This was a Christian school, after all.

Amidst this chaos, one of my teachers challenged us to pray fervently for grace, mercy, and miracles. He begged us to intercede for the ministry, pray for revival, and purpose to be true examples of Christ. He said God was looking for a Daniel."

Mr. Pierce paused. He lowered his head and sighed. "For a while, I took on that challenge. I was determined to be a prayer warrior; but it interfered too much with my way of life, my dreams. I tried to get my friends to join me, but no one wanted to. Even my family told me that I was going overboard. After a few months, I gave up. Surely God was entitled to help after my weeks of sacrifice. The school closed after graduation that year. I can still acutely remember my Bible teacher's tears that night. His challenge had not fallen on deaf ears, just unwilling ones. I knew that I had made the worst decision of my life."

Daniel's attention was fully riveted on Mr. Pierce. He saw wrinkles scar the man's brow as he relived his past. All thoughts of ridiculing his reminiscing fled from Daniel's mind as the former principal continued speaking.

"Not long after, the state bought the school property and reopened it as a charter academy. Almost out of guilt and in an attempt to fix my mistakes, I came back to teach math. I shared Christ with those I could. Eventually, I was elected principal. Until this year, I've been able to keep Christ present on campus. These hands of mine have never been clasped in prayer more than they have this year." Mr. Pierce looked directly at Daniel, his eyes soft with tears. "We needed a Daniel then, just like we need one now. God is always on time, but we never seem to be listening when He calls. Too often, we stop praying too early. I can't help but wonder what would have happened if I had kept praying. Nothing? Possibly. Something big? More than likely. If only I had kept falling at the throne of grace and begging God to intervene." Mr. Pierce put his hands into his jacket pocket. "Chancellor is in even worse shape than it was. Do you suppose God's looking for another Daniel now?"

Daniel pulled his gaze away from Mr. Pierce. He balled his fist around that single blade of grass even tighter. He felt his heart beat double time. "What does that have to do with me?"

Mr. Pierce chuckled. "Who said it has anything to do with you? I was referring to the biblical Daniel. I'm just an old man sharing my thoughts."

Mr. Pierce took a small, folded piece of paper from his pocket and placed it on Daniel's knee. He stood and gently squeezed Daniel's shoulder. "Find someone to share your thoughts with, Son. It's really helpful."

As abruptly as he had appeared, Mr. Pierce began to walk away. Daniel could barely breathe. He looked at the paper on his knee. Slowly, he reached for it and opened it while still clinging to that single blade of grass. Scrawled on the inside were four words.

I'm praying for you.

Daniel gasped. He looked across the field, wanting to call Mr. Pierce back as questions welled up inside of him. The old man was already part of the mass of pedestrians who gave neither Chancellor nor Daniel a second glance. Daniel shivered as he lowered his gaze to the ground beneath his feet. He opened his palm and the last blade of grass flew from his hand. Daniel shook his head.

"You know I want to quit, don't You God?"

There was no answer. He couldn't bear more unanswered prayers. They were the most unnerving aspects about his Father. He scratched his chin and looked up at the sky.

"I asked You to help me find a sanctuary here, without Mom, not chaos."

In the silence, a psalm came to Daniel's mind. *The name of the Lord is a strong tower: the righteous runneth into it, and is safe.*

He rubbed his face. He glanced at Chancellor's building. A Christian school? A place where foundations had been built to glorify Christ? Where were those foundations now?

Right here.

The unbidden response came to Daniel. He shook his head, closed his eyes, and rested his head in his hands.

No! I'm done God. I gave up my dreams to make a difference and only have empty hands left. I can't give You those too. I'm tired. I can't make the difference anymore. I want to belong somewhere.

The wind picked up. Daniel felt it seep through his clothes and threaten to blow him away. He braced himself against it. As it died down, he was aware of a new warmth descending upon him. He tentatively opened his eyes. The sight that met him took his breath away.

In the sky, forecasted to be completely overcast, a single ray of sunshine shot through the clouds and bathed him in light. The clouds that surrounded that ray were lined in gold, completing the majestic morning display. Daniel's jaw dropped. Had he just rejected this God? This God Who cared enough to send His broken child a small ray of sunshine? This God Who had given His empty hands to be scarred for the world? This God Who had allowed Chancellor's foundations to be erected here in hopes that His people would build it up? This God Who remained even when a community, an entire nation, tried to push Him away? Was this the One he had just refused to surrender his empty hands to?

Daniel gasped. He did belong to something, but it was something much bigger than the fists and words and laws of Chancellor High. He belonged to a kingdom which was void of orphans, just as he had boldly declared in his speech before the recruiters. He closed his eyes. When had his focus become so skewed?

If the foundations be destroyed, what can the righteous do?

Daniel knew one thing that he could do.

He slipped from the bleachers onto the damp ground. With his face toward the rising sun, he lifted his thoughts to the Intercessor Who promised to recognize His children to the Father.

"Lord God, search my heart, renew my mind. Please, take my pride and rebellion from me and fill me with Your Holy Spirit. I have been so concerned about finding a comfort zone and living for my dreams that I have lost sight of You. O my God, Chancellor is not mine to work in, it is solely Yours. It has always been Yours. Lord, the lions are roaring. I beg you to close their mouths and open their eyes and hearts. Lord, show me what Your dream is. O my Saviour, what is Your dream?"

Daniel lifted tear-filled eyes. From his prostrate view on the field, the minute details of the Georgian soil and mown grass filled his vision. He shifted his eyes to the expanse before him. The field was filled; but this time, there were no fans cheering him on. On the sun-soaked area, he saw Chancellor's students, watching, waiting, wondering why Daniel was on the field. Behind them, the American flag waved allowing a few glances of Trinity's steeple parallel to it. Daniel looked beyond the field's gate to the street. Only a small walkway separated Chancellor from Trinity. It was such a small gap which needed to be closed for God to enter the school. How many more students were beyond Chancellor, waiting and lacking all that God had to offer? God's dream had to begin somewhere.

Daniel fell to the ground again. A peace filled him as he surrendered Chancellor's past, present, and future to God. There was a gap that needed to be filled. He would gladly stand in that gap, with empty hands but a full heart. This time, he wouldn't do it alone. God was going to have to be the One to do the work. Daniel's only responsibility was to stand. He sighed and smiled against the ground. It was time for the world to see what God could do with a dream.

†

Neala waited until she heard her mother settling down in the kitchen with her cup of tea. She took a deep breath. Roy was gone.

This was the only chance she'd have. She stepped out of her room and walked toward the dining room.

She found her mother in her usual place, sipping tea at the head of their small dining table. She glanced over a stack of brochures. Her mother looked much better than she had this morning. As Neala approached her in the dim light, fear threatened to stop her. A sense of peace transcended that fear and prodded her forward. This was where the search must begin.

Jane looked up as Neala settled beside her. She pushed one of the brochures under her elbow. "Neala? I thought you were in bed."

She cleared her throat. "I was."

Jane nodded and took another sip from her mug. The tick tock of the kitchen clock and passing cars were the only sounds in the house. When was the last time they had sat across from each other without harsh words between them? Neala reveled in it for a moment. She bit her lower lip.

"I need to tell you something," she began, "It's a decision I've made." Neala gave her mother a crooked smile. "You might not like it."

She paused to give her mother a chance to start raving. To her surprise, Jane instead set down her cup of tea and gave Neala her full attention. Was her mother listening?

She cleared her throat. "Mom, I'm...I'm going back to Trinity. I'm not going to say that Trinity needs me, but I need what Trinity has to offer. I need to know Who God really is, for me. Lately, I've seen such sacrifice in God's name, and it both confuses and compels me. I need to know the God Who died on the cross. I want to know if it's true that He died for me."

Neala took a deep breath and waited. Now it was coming. Now the peace would be shattered. She searched her mother's gaze for a temper. Instead, she found a sheen of tears. Jane smiled.

"Where has my little girl gone?" she whispered. "I can't cuddle with you anymore. You are a grown woman making decisions for yourself. I respect that, Sweetheart."

She took a moment to make sure she had heard correctly. "You do?"

Jane nodded. "I can't stop you; I know that now. But I'm glad you shared your decision with me. Go find God, Neala." Jane paused. She looked down at the brochures in her hand. With a sigh, she looked back up at Neala, "Now, I have something I want to share with you." She looked away from Neala and back at the pile of papers on the table. A small tear dripped down her cheek.

Neala frowned. "Are you okay?"

Jane quickly wiped the tear away. She shook her head, glancing up with a weak smile. "Oh, it's nothing you need to worry about."

"You know, you don't always have to be the strong one, Mom."

Jane laughed. "There you go, being all grown up again." She took a deep breath, then cleared her throat. "It's just, Roy and I had another argument again. It was bad this time. He's not what I expected him to be…"

Her voice trailed off as she stared off into the distance. Neala swallowed hard. What had Roy said this time? Why did her mom keep holding on to him?

Jane turned back toward Neala. "I want more kids, Neala. So badly but Roy…he told me this morning he'd rather die first. He doesn't want to be tied down. Marriage is enough of a tether…"

"He literally called marriage a tether? Really Mom? Is that what you want to be to him?"

"Oh Neala, he's helping me pay the bills. I owe him."

"You owe him nothing."

"I wish that were true." Her hands trembled as she pushed back her red curls. "I just didn't expect this from him. I don't know what to do. I thought we were in a good place."

Neala nodded slowly. "Sooo, you still want to marry him?"

Jane groaned. "I don't know."

"Well, it's been my experience that if you love someone you want to make that person happy." Neala swallowed a lump in her throat. This was no time to think about how she'd wronged The Crusaders. This was time to think of her mom. "It sounds like Roy only wants to please himself. You are an amazing person, Mom. Don't let him bring you down. Don't settle for half the love that you deserve."

Jane nodded slowly. "Do you think maybe, with all your God searching, you could ask your church friends to pray for me? I want to make the best decision for us."

Neala nodded. "I would love to." She cocked her head. "Mom, I'm not looking for God just for myself. You could come with me to Trinity. Roy is usually busy all Sunday morning."

Jane tucked a stray piece of hair behind her ear. "I wouldn't know how to act in church."

Neala shrugged. "Just go and listen."

With a sigh, she reached over to squeeze her daughter's hand. "I will think about it."

Neala swallowed hard. Her mother's gentle touch was more than she could bear. She clasped her mother's hand and squeezed back. How was it that talking about God had compelled Jane to finally reach out to her daughter? Neala's desire to understand Him grew more. Maybe God was exactly what this family needed.

CHAPTER 23
CHANGED

Coach Mackenzie furrowed his brow. He slid the State folder closer to him. With his fingers, he pried off a sticky note lying on top of it. He squinted in the dim light to read the words written on it.

I'll be praying for you.

He leaned back in his chair. His eyes glanced at the bottom drawer of his desk. It was the one drawer Principal Wilkins never looked in. Coach Mackenzie opened the drawer. He caught sight of the black book in the bottom and sighed.

After a few seconds, he lifted the book and stuffed it in his briefcase. He placed the sticky note inside and zipped up the case. Glancing around his office, he reached for his folder and began filling out a few more sheets about the Conqueror team. Perhaps tonight, after his work was done, he would take a peek into his favorite childhood book. Perhaps then he'd call his father and ask about bringing the kids over for Sunday School. Perhaps.

†

Daniel took a deep breath. He pressed against the door as he turned the doorknob. It opened noiselessly. He stepped across a familiar threshold. Laughter and voices filtered out of Art's living room. With new eyes, he took an appreciative glance at his haven, his sanctuary. He paused just outside the arch that opened up into their Bible study area and smiled. Three faithful friends motioned excitedly through the air as Randy shook his head and smiled in return. Had he really abandoned them for a full month? Daniel stepped forward bringing a cloud of silence with him. He swallowed.

"Hey," he said.

For a moment no one answered. Daniel tightened his hold on his Bible. He had surrendered everything to God. What if he took them too? Art stepped up and gave him a short embrace. The others followed in unison.

"Good to have you back, Brother."

"Good to be back."

Randy crossed his arms. "Where exactly have you been, Man?"

Daniel took a deep breath. He lowered his backpack to the ground. "I'd actually like to tell you. If I can."

The Crusaders all sat in their respective places. Instead of sitting with them, Daniel kept his place in the center of the living room floor. He swallowed hard.

"I'm sorry I've been out for so long, but at the same time I'm not. God has been working on my heart. God has given me a new vision that I want to share with you. A vision for Chancellor High." He reached for the Bible in his backpack. He flipped to the verse he had marked earlier that morning. His voice trembled a little as he read it aloud. "…The effectual fervent prayer of a righteous man availeth much."

Daniel lowered his Bible. He looked at the four Crusaders who surrounded him. Would they share his vision? Would they all understand? There was only one way to find out. He had to share what God had shared with him.

"There are four months of school left. After that, we will leave Chancellor High and probably never come back. What will be left is the mark we leave behind. I believe God wants to bring revival to Chancellor High. I want to get as many students to follow Christ as possible before I leave those school walls. I don't want to leave without knowing that I've tried my best, but I can't do it alone. I'm just Daniel." Daniel paused. His eyes fell on the verse he had just read and he smiled. "The only hope for Chancellor High is revival in God's people, namely those at Trinity. And the only way for revival is prayer."

Daniel looked back at The Crusaders. "Guys, God promises that '…The effectual fervent prayer of a righteous man availeth much.' Now, imagine what the fervent prayer of many righteous men could do." He shook his head. "For a while now, I thought that I had to bear this burden alone." Daniel smiled. "But that is why God gave me The Crusaders." He nodded. "I want to suggest that, for the next two months, we pray for salvation for the unsaved and for revival in both Trinity and Chancellor. I mean, all-out, fervent and specific prayer. We can't rebel against the authority, but we can bring down Satan's walls with prayer. Are you willing to pray with me?"

For a moment, the room was completely silent. Each Crusader gazed at his Bible, reading the verse he had just shared. Daniel did the same, praying that they would listen. Finally, Art spoke.

"Daniel, I've been praying for the same thing for months now."

Daniel felt his heart jump. Sean and Matthew nodded in agreement. Randy smirked. "Well, I haven't thought that much about it, but I'm more than willing to start now."

Art shook his head. "You know, Daniel, I think God might know that we're getting tired praying alone. I suppose it's time to join forces and create a mob that will fall at God's throne and beg for revival."

Daniel smiled and nodded. Relief flowed through him. When God gave a dream, He certainly gave all the resources needed to accomplish it.

Together, they all took out a piece of paper and began to write down specific people who they knew were unsaved. They listed members in Trinity and areas they saw that needed improvement in both Chancellor and Trinity. When they were done, they placed their papers in a circle and knelt beside them. Familiar names were on both lists: salvation for Neala, Garcia, Crystal, the teachers and staff, and, on the top of each list, Principal Wilkins. If revival was going to start in Chancellor, it had to start with its leader. Once they finished their lists, The Crusaders began to pray.

†

Neala rubbed her eyes. It was too early, way too early. Still, she couldn't spend another minute tossing and turning in bed. What was this restlessness she couldn't shake?

After getting a glass of water, she walked back into her room. With a sigh, she reached for her laptop and climbed back into bed. As the computer started up, Neala looked around her dark room.

The calendar on the left wall above her bed had this date marked as her mother's day for pregnancy support at Trinity. She leaned back, accidentally knocking *Les Misérables* from beneath her pillow and onto the ground. She paused, waiting for an indication that the sound of the book hitting the ground had not spooked her mother and Roy.

When she was sure that all was silent, she moved her laptop beside her and leaned down to pick it up. A small folded paper fell out of it. She picked it up and unfolded it. The Crusaders. Neala folded the paper in half again. She closed her eyes. How long had it been since she'd gone to Bible study? Two weeks? She opened the front cover of *Les Misérables* to place the paper inside it again.

Just as she was about to close the book, she noticed some words written on the back portion of the paper. Curious, she brought the paper close to her laptop and used its light to read the words.

I'm praying for you.

Neala cocked her head. *Daniel?* Just today, everyone had been talking about how all of the prayer notes had stopped. This one was from Daniel and could not be recent, not with *Les Misérables* being hidden so well under her pillow. She bit her lower lip. She'd been able to avoid all of The Crusaders with her mom having to go home so quickly after services. Still, here was Daniel's message. She took a deep breath. It was time to go back to step one. She opened the Internet and found her link to the Crusader blogspot. Tentatively, she clicked on it.

The sheer number of updates that popped onto the screen were a big reminder of how much Neala had missed. She scrolled through the home page, stopping short when she saw a video of Daniel posted on his wall. It was entitled "Scholarship Speech." Beneath the video, comments ranged from "epitome of idiocy" and "your journey could have had a better end" to "awesome" and "show them exactly Who God is." Neala poised her mouse cursor over the video.

What had Daniel said that night before he came to rescue her from Elliot? Had he won the scholarship? The results would not be announced until the summer, but this video would tell her enough for her to figure it out on her own. She clicked the play button.

The moment Daniel started his speech, Neala knew he was the best candidate for the scholarship. As he continued, however, the comments about the video made sense. She leaned back in her bed, eyes wide, as she watched Daniel pull out different colored cloths and lay them across the podium.

He was sharing the Gospel with the audience. He wasn't doing it out of malice, which was clear from the way his eyes shone as he continued through the points of the Gospel. Instead, he was doing it out of love. The recruiters had asked him to share the important things of his life, and he did.

Neala listened carefully to his speech. With each new cloth he pulled out, Neala felt something moving in her heart.

As his speech came to a close, one phrase caught her attention. Through this love...Neala pressed the pause button. She was surprised to find herself panting. She pushed back hair from her face.

For God so loved the world...

So, Daniel hadn't gotten the scholarship. She looked at the five cloths covering the podium in Chancellor's gymnasium. This was why everyone at Chancellor had treated him so badly after the winter party. Daniel had praised God instead of the realm of soccer on the night of the scholarship ceremony. And he had still had time to lead her home?

Those were the true colors of Daniel's faith. He had given up soccer for Christ and turned to open his arms to her.

For God so loved the world...

Neala bolted out of bed. She began pacing the floor. The colors of redemption raced through her mind. She shook her head. No. This gift wasn't for her. This love couldn't be hers. Her emptiness and darkness was as black as the cloth that hung first on the podium. Why then was her heart racing at the thought that the darkness could be wiped away?

Her eyes gazed at the laptop screen again. She felt tears come to her eyes as she caught sight of the red cloth, right in the center of the podium Daniel stood behind. It looked very much like a swath of scarlet blood.

For God so loved the world, Neala. The whole world.

Neala cupped her hands and looked down at her empty palms. Could Christ have really died for her too? She was the biggest part of the world. Everything she said and did was of the world. But, Daniel had held out his hands, so many months ago and shown her a cure. He had asked her to take it. She remembered her response. Someday. Now, Neala wondered how long it would take for that someday. What if she never allowed for that someday? Would she slip away in this state of emptiness? Didn't Christ's blood mean anything to her? It meant everything to Daniel.

Neala trembled. She glanced up at Daniel's paused video again. She remembered her statement to her mother two weeks ago. *I want to know Who God is for me.* And her mother's response: "Go find God, Neala."

Neala froze as a wave of understanding washed over her. She thought that she had to go out, somewhere in a deep contemplative understanding, and find God on her own. And yet, here He was. Here He stood in Daniel and here He stood in her room waiting for her. God could not be found; God had to find her. And He had. What would Neala do now? Would she reach for Him or ignore Him?

Neala closed her eyes against the lies she'd heard from Reganne and her friends. Those words didn't matter. Those lies had not stopped

178

God from saving Neala through Daniel on the worst night of her life. They hadn't stopped her from finding her way to Trinity again. A wave of doubt rose up in her mind and she shook her head. No. Doubts and fears were not going to win. Not today.

She took a deep breath. She tucked her knees under her, folded her hands and lowered her head. She paused. How was she supposed to start? As a tear escaped her eyelids, she opened her mouth. It sounded small compared to the wave of love washing over her.

"God, I'm not sure where to start. You know who I am. You've seen me struggling to run away from You and Your Son so many times. The thing is, I don't understand Your kind of love. But I don't think I'm supposed to." Neala cleared her throat. "I guess, what I'm trying to say is that I'm ready to believe on Your Son now. I'm…I'm ready to accept His blood. Jesus, please cleanse my filthy heart of all my sin and make me a new creation as You promised You would in Your Word. I believe that You died and rose from the dead to prepare a place for Your believers and, for that reason, please take me to Heaven when I enter into eternity. Raise me from the emptiness I've been living in and fill me with You. In Jesus' name, Amen."

Neala didn't realize she was crying until after the prayer. She felt something shift in her heart. Something different moved within her and wrapped around her. She opened her eyes.

She wasn't empty. No, Neala Baptiste was not empty; but instead, in place of the emptiness, she felt a song welling up inside of her. Neala jumped to her feet. Smiling, she shuffled through her backpack and grabbed a few blank, musical composition sheets. With trembling fingers, she wrote the day's date above the music lines. Then, she wrote the first note of her forbidden song. It was the song that had oppressed her on so many nights with its haunting and hopeless ending. But this morning, it carried a new light. As she positioned notes across the page, she knew this wasn't her song anymore. This was God's song, and He had given her a new ending.

†

"Daniel?"

Daniel lifted his tear-stained face as his aunt and uncle entered his room. He smiled and rose from his knees. Wiping the tears from his eyes, he cleared his throat. This was going to be awkward. He reached for the doorknob of his closet and opened it. His aunt and uncle stood in the doorway, gaping at the sight of his head popping out of his closet.

"Yes?"

Aunt Lisa glanced at Uncle Devon. They stared at each other silently before looking back at Daniel. Uncle Devon scratched his chin.

"It's five o' clock in the morning, Daniel. Are you all right? We heard you shouting."

Daniel sighed. He climbed out of the closet and walked over toward his bed. He lowered himself onto his bed, wiping both tears and sweat from his face. He nodded slowly. "I'm fine now. I...I was just praying."

Aunt Lisa and Uncle Devon glanced between each other. He shook his head at the sight.

"What?" he said. "Prayer is warfare right?"

Uncle Devon sat across from Daniel and narrowed his eyes. "You were praying in your closet?"

Daniel smiled. "Hey, I have Scripture to back it up." When neither of his guardians laughed, he sighed. "Mom and I used to do that. When I was little and I was afraid that there were monsters in the closet, we would climb in together and pray them away. Then, when she got sick, I prayed the monster of cancer away on my own, in my closet." He looked down at the palm of his hands. "It's where I do my battles." He glanced up at Aunt Lisa. "I fight Satan in my closet."

Aunt Lisa bit her lower lip and looked down. Uncle Devon sighed. He leaned back in Daniel's chair and gazed at Daniel as if trying to figure out if he was telling the truth.

"What monsters were you fighting today?"

Daniel turned his face to the window. The morning was still dark. "I woke up this morning and felt a burden to start praying for Neala. She's one of the girls in our youth group."

Aunt Lisa nodded. "Yes, her mother is in my pregnancy support group. She brought you home the other night, didn't she?"

Daniel nodded. "Look, all I know is that this morning I had to pray for her. I felt as if maybe God was telling me that she was fighting her own battle somewhere, and I didn't want Satan to get a hold of her during her battle. So I got in my closet and prayed." Daniel leaned against his pillows. "It was a long battle."

Aunt Lisa stepped out from behind Uncle Devon. She sat on the edge of Daniel's bed. Pulling his blanket out from under his feet, she draped it over him. Tears filled her eyes. "Did you win?" she whispered.

Daniel smiled, his eyes closed in exhaustion. "God did."

CHAPTER 24
REVIVAL

Pastor Moore's secretary looked him straight in the eyes. "We can't afford this evangelist."

Pastor Moore ran a hand over his face. It was always about the money. He shook his head. "We don't have to afford him. Freddie Harton has agreed to hold a revival for nothing more than a place to stay and good food to eat. The food might cost a fortune though." He winked at his secretary, thinking of the last time he had seen the plump and vigorous evangelist. That had been quite a few years back. Would Harton be as gray as Pastor Moore was now? He averted his attention to his secretary, who frowned at him.

"Why would Harton do that?"

"Because, despite what most members of Trinity Baptist Church think, there are still people out there whose greatest desire is to see the Gospel spread, not their pockets filled. We are going to give him all that we have." Pastor Moore gazed at his reflection in his shiny oak desk. He looked just about as old as his father had. "And we are going to hope that the 'whirlwind' he's so famous for comes through Trinity's walls."

The secretary sighed. "We don't need revival, Pastor Moore."

He glanced up. The very statement took his breath away. He took the Evangelist Harton's phone number from his secretary's hands and looked her straight in the eyes. "For that very reason, we do."

†

"What do you think," whispered Art. "Do you think it's the answer to our prayers?"

Daniel glanced around Trinity's auditorium. Stiff-necked couples and careless individuals sat in their normal places. Despite the evangelist's strong sermon this morning, the altars had been empty again. Daniel saw the heaviness in Pastor Moore's eyes as it came to an end. It might take longer than two months for something to change in this area. His eyes fell on a handful of students from Chancellor who had responded to his revival invitation when he met them in the drugstore this afternoon. They whispered and pointed every time a member entered, making the congregation squirm. Daniel sighed.

"Only God knows," he said to Art, "but I'm not sure what to think about it."

Just as Daniel was turning around, Sean nudged him in the side and motioned toward the back with his head. "Hey, look," he whispered.

Daniel turned in time to see Randy walk into the auditorium. He paused, turned, and motioned at someone from the door. Almost as if they were being dragged by an invisible force, Garcia walked into the auditorium followed by a handful of Conqueror soccer players. They filed into the very back of the auditorium.

Daniel smiled as Randy leaned over to speak to them. They glanced around at the regular church people, comparing their Sunday best to their own ripped and baggy jeans and large T-shirts. A few of them crossed their arms and glared defiantly at the disgusted church members. Daniel gave them a little wave. Garcia was the only one to respond, waving vigorously in his direction. Of all the soccer players, Garcia and The Crusaders were the only ones who had missed him on the soccer team. Randy motioned to Daniel to let him know that he was going to sit with his guests. Daniel nodded and faced forward.

As the piano music began to play, he lifted the tip of his Bible cover. Inside, he tucked a small note card that he found on his dresser this morning. It had been written by Aunt Lisa.

Forget what I told you about moderation.
Show the world Who God is, Daniel.

Daniel smiled as he reached for the hymnbook and joined the congregation in worship. Revival could come one step at a time.

When Evangelist Harton stepped up to the pulpit, he greeted the congregation with a facial expression that had quickly become his trademark: a radiant smile, kind of like the calm before the storm. He laid his Bible on the pulpit and looked down at the congregation. His booming voice filled the auditorium.

"How are y'all doing tonight? Well, I'm going to assume that everyone is doing quite well since the altars were empty this morning. Amen?"

No one in the congregation responded. They glanced at one another, eyes wide. Daniel swallowed hard, praying in the back of his mind. The evangelist cleared his throat.

"Now, tonight, I'm going to jump right into the message. This morning I did break the ice with jokes and gave you a good abdominal workout." A few of the girls in front of Daniel giggled. Evangelist Harton opened his Bible. "Please join me in the book of Amos and we're going to read a few passages there throughout the night; but right now, let's just read the first verse of this book. And the Bible says 'The words of Amos, who was among the herdmen of Tekoa, which he saw concerning Israel in the days of Uzziah king of Judah, and in the days of Jeroboam the son of Joash king of Israel, two years before the earthquake.' Now, tonight, I want to speak on the subject of 'When God's People Refuse Revival.'" Evangelist Harton paused to lead the congregation in prayer. When he was done, he began his sermon.

He spoke of how God used a simple herdsman to bring revival to people who refused it. Daniel hung onto every word, feeling the truth of God using the "simple" for his glory. He emphasized the greed of holding back the blessings God gave to his people.

"The thing is, most of us have hoarded that gift of salvation and all the joy it brings to ourselves," said the evangelist. "We daren't share it with somebody else. Why would God ask it of us?"

185

Daniel swallowed hard. *Lord, don't ever let me hoard Your blessings.*

Art shifted next to him as the evangelist spoke of the spiritual apathy in the chapter of Scripture. Each word he spoke hit like a blow to Daniel's heart. He knew too well what it was like to depend on himself instead of God, to hold back and refuse to give in because of pride. The Spirit plucked his heart and he listened.

I never want to hold back my spirit from You again.

Near the close of the message, the evangelist spoke about the effects of spiritual famine.

"All you have to do is take a step outside, and you can see the results of spiritual famine in our nation."

Daniel thought about Neala on the dock and his vision of Chancellor High. Tears clouded his eyes. *I can't ever forget that vision.*

"God sent Amos before the earthquake, before the judgment, to open their eyes. He was giving them one last chance before the earthquake. Trinity Baptist Church, is it going to take an earthquake to move God's people?"

Daniel's breath caught in his throat. Sometimes it did. Sometimes God had to take everything away to make room for His plan. He clasped his hands together. As much as it was in his power, he would do whatever it took to make sure that never happened here or at Chancellor High.

The closing for the invitation came with the evangelist's final words. "Will you come now, or are you going to force God to send an earthquake?"

The invitation opened with the traditional piano playing. Daniel rose to his feet, consumed by the vision of a thirsty student body. This time, when he reached the altar, he found very little room to kneel. It seemed as if the entire congregation had finally found their feet and used them to run to the altar. The sound of sobbing caught his attention, and Daniel watched dumbfounded as a line of Conqueror soccer players approached Evangelist Harton who was leading a ring of people to salvation. He fell to his knees, at a loss for words. His heart was full. It had come. It really had come. He trembled at the realization. Trinity was waking up.

CHAPTER 25
ANSWERED

Coach Mackenzie found only ten soccer players at Friday night practice. This was the first practice to prepare them for the State. These results weren't good. They couldn't win if none of the players showed up. He blew his whistle to call the ten players to the benches. Once they were seated, he frowned.

"I want to know where the rest of our team is. If you know, please speak up."

For a moment, no one spoke. Then, Elliot spat on the ground and pointed across the field. "They are at Trinity. There is some big revival or something going on." Elliot cursed under his breath.

Coach Mackenzie gazed across the field to the small white church building. His soccer players were at church? That was the last place he'd imagine they'd end up. He scratched his head. What was going on? He sighed. Principal Wilkins wouldn't be pleased with this report. He shook his head and turned back to the ten soccer players in front of him. There was no need to worry. Revivals never lasted more than a week. By Monday, he'd have his team back, and Chancellor would still win in soccer.

†

The church was crowded. Tonight was Youth Friday, and everyone gathered to hear the final strains of Trinity's revival. Daniel filed in with the rest of the youth choir and picked up his songbook. From the back, Neala moved forward and took her place at the piano. Daniel could feel the Spirit moving already. He caught hold of Pastor Moore's eyes and smiled. He couldn't help but wonder what God had planned for tonight.

The service began with the teenagers singing "Sanctuary." Then, after a few announcements and fellowship, the teen choir sang one more song: "I Have Been Blessed." Daniel looked around. He caught sight of Randy and Garcia in the back of the auditorium. Garcia still wore his baggy pants and graphic t-shirts, but at least he was attempting to fix his hair occasionally. Randy's renewed devotion continued to grow every day. He smiled at Daniel now. Aunt Lisa and Uncle Devon had begun to join him in his daily prayers for Chancellor. The entire congregation had a new spirit about them. Daniel sang the words to the song with gusto. Yes, he truly had been blessed. He now had a home.

After the special, the teen choir filed out of the choir loft. It wasn't until Daniel was seated in the second row reserved for the teenage guys that he noticed one of the teenagers had stayed on the stage. Neala walked toward the small piano and laid a few sheets of music on the music bracket. Then she approached a microphone set up on the side of the pulpit. He could see her fingers tremble as she cleared her throat. The congregation around Daniel stirred and whispers echoed throughout the auditorium.

"What's the rebel doing up there?"

"Why is the pastor allowing this?"

"I can't believe she's speaking!"

Daniel leaned forward, pushing away the voices that protested. Let them break the spirit of revival; he wanted to know what God had planned. His heart leapt when she glanced at him. She took a deep breath, got a nod from Pastor Moore, and then spoke.

"What is grace?" she began. "I have struggled with that question for years now. I began attending Trinity Youth Group five years ago. My mom thought it would be a good attitude adjuster." Neala laughed nervously. She swallowed hard. "I always enjoyed coming and listening to lessons and principles from the Bible, but there was one story I never understood: the story of the cross. How could an all-powerful God send His Son to die for the world? Why would His Son be willing to die for someone...someone like me? And, if His redemption was so transforming, why did so many people who claimed His name seem less Christ-like than the worldliest friends I knew? Why weren't they out there showing us in the world what it was like to live in light of that redemption?"

People in the room shifted. Neala lowered her eyes. For a few moments, Daniel wondered if she would walk away. But then, she lifted her eyes. A small smile graced her lips.

"Then, in September, God showed me a measure of grace through a friend. This friend taught me what grace and sacrifice meant. Through him, I saw facets of Jesus I had never seen before. I saw corners of my world change due to his actions, and he awakened in me a desire to go beyond scratching the surface of faith in God and really find out Who his God was. I know through it all that he was praying for me."

Neala looked straight at Daniel. Her eyes were clear and bright, but he felt as if her smile were meant for someone beyond him. The next words she spoke left him breathless.

"Last weekend, I accepted Christ as my personal Saviour." Neala laughed at the silence in the auditorium. She wiped away tears that had begun to fall unbidden down both of her cheeks. "And you know what, I now am beginning to understand the cross and grace. I now understand that it's not about me being worthy or good enough; it's about how compassionate my Jesus is. Grace is...grace is God's love."

She bit her lower lip and fought for composure. A few whispered amens filtered through the auditorium. In his seat, Daniel battled overwhelming emotions. Finally, Neala cleared her throat.

"I have always had a passion for music; and ever since I came here five years ago, a song has been battling its way within me. I've been so afraid to write it because the end had no hope. After I got saved, I had to write it with a different ending. I'd like to play this song for you today. It's about my journey to Amazing Grace."

Without further adieu, Neala approached the piano bench. With trembling hands, she began playing a compilation Daniel recognized. It was the song he had accidentally overheard so many months ago. It was the secret compilation of "Danny Boy" and "Amazing Grace" that told of a lonely girl on a long and lonely road to peace. At the end, however, Neala had added the final triumphant notes of "Amazing Grace" with the final notes of "Danny Boy" fading in the light of eternal victory.

Daniel felt the swell and tide of the music speaking to him and those around him. God had brought her home. Some of the girls who had sneered and rebuffed Neala wiped tears from their eyes and closed their eyes in prayer. As Daniel witnessed the radiance on Neala's tearstained face, he could think of only one thing.

Thank You, my God, my Saviour, my King. Thank You for saving Neala. Thank You for the power that breaks Satan's chains.

When Neala finished, Daniel was the first to applaud. The room turned into an uproar, and many of them stood to welcome Neala into God's family. She began sobbing on the piano bench and laughing at the same time. Mrs. Timberlake and a few of the youth group girls met and embraced her at the altar.

Daniel caught Neala's shining eyes. She mouthed a "thank you" to him. Daniel could only nod and wipe away his own tears. He gazed in wonder into the eyes of an answered prayer.

CHAPTER 26
SECRETS

Principal Wilkins smiled at the letter before him. This was good news and bad news all wrapped in one. He glanced at the calendar. So, his soccer players were getting religion, huh? More than likely Daniel had something to do with it. Well, he would just have to put an end to it. He logged into his administrative email account and pulled up a new email template. This year, Chancellor was going to be different. Sponsor the National Day of Prayer on the soccer field? Well, the schedule was about to change.

†

The Crusaders sat in Pastor Moore's office, waiting. Mr. Pierce stood behind them as he perused the paper they'd laid before him. As he contemplated the message, Daniel thought about the words on that page that were now imprinted on his mind although he had received it only an hour earlier.

Dear Parents and Student Body,
     Every year, Chancellor sponsors the National Day of Prayer on the soccer field as an act of community service. Due to the religious connotations of this act, however, I have moved to cancel this National Day of

Prayer as it mixes church and state and is against the new school policy. I have already informed the mayor of this change. I am sending this email to avoid inconvenience for those who have planned to attend this year. If you have any questions, feel free to contact Chancellor's secretary. -Principal Wilkins

With a sigh, Pastor Moore sat back in his chair. He glanced up at the four young men seated in his office. He shook his head.

"I'm surprised the mayor allowed him to cancel it. Chancellor's National Day of Prayer has always been a highlight to bring the community together."

Daniel glanced at Art. He took a deep breath. "Sir, there is a reason we brought this to you today."

Pastor Moore grinned. "I thought there might be." He looked up at Mr. Pierce. "Especially since you brought one of my deacons with you."

Daniel looked up at Mr. Pierce. He motioned toward Pastor Moore and nodded. Daniel clasped his hands together. "When I got the memo, I thought it was another closed door. Then, I realized it might be an open window."

Pastor Moore furrowed his brow. "What do you mean?"

"What if we held the National Day of Prayer here at Trinity?"

Pastor Moore's eyes widened. He rubbed his jaw. "It's possible that God has been preparing Trinity for this with the revival last month and the new passion in the members to spread the Gospel. We could open the altars on May 6 and open our doors to those in need."

Randy spoke up. "We've been praying about it all week in Bible study. I think this is exactly what Trinity needs."

Sean held up his hands. "Now, we do need to keep some separation, so we were thinking of passing out flyers and also some prayer request cards for the next three weeks so that those who can't come could send in their requests."

Pastor Moore leaned forward. "We could then divide the prayer requests with a willing group of Trinity's members."

192

Daniel nodded. He kept Pastor Moore's gaze, searching and questioning at the same time. Pastor Moore chuckled and looked up at Mr. Pierce.

"We would be running the race of faith at Trinity's altar."

Daniel grinned. "Kind of like a prayer-a-thon."

Pastor Moore raised his eyebrows. "A prayer-a-thon. That's exactly what it would be."

All of the heads nodded in unison. Pastor Moore put his hand on his Bible. He thought of the sticky note still pasted on the inside cover. For months, someone already had been praying for Trinity. A revival had resulted and now this venue of ministry. He closed his eyes for a second. Was this the right path to take? The peace that passeth all understanding washed over him. He looked up and smiled at the group of teens and the elderly man that waited for his answer. He nodded.

"On Sunday, we will distribute the flyers. Trinity is going to have a prayer-a-thon."

†

"Neala. Come here!"

Neala pressed her cell phone closer to her ear. Not only did she have Reganne in hysterics over the phone, but now Roy was calling her to the living room. Since when had they observed early "family" meetings? Since when had he known that Neala even existed in the same household? She winced as Reganne continued to speak.

"Tell me Elliot was just kidding, Neala. He said that the reason you've been skipping out on us these last few weeks is because you've been doing some church thing. Tell me you're not turning into some religious freak like Randy."

She sighed. "Reganne, there is no freakiness involved. God found me. I'm saved now, so I won't be doing the same Sunday afternoon and Friday night stuff with the gang. I'm...I'm different."

Reganne responded with silence. Neala waited, wondering if she had hung up. She finally spoke, the sound of tears in her voice. "Look, I already lost Randy. I'm not willing to lose you. Get a grip."

Neala bit her lower lip. "You're not losing me, Reganne. I'm still here. I'm just new. God made me new. Maybe…maybe I can talk to you about it today at lunch."

"If you can find a seat. Goodbye, Neala."

Neala pressed the end button and dropped the phone in her lap. She closed her eyes. Why did it have to be like this? Why did she have to lose her friends to have a new testimony? She glanced at the wall clock. She would have to mention it in Bible study this morning. She wanted Reganne to know this true freedom in Christ. It went beyond becoming freaky. It was about being freed from sin. She bent down to grab her backpack, her heart heavy over Reganne.

"Neala!"

She jumped. She had forgotten about Roy. She slung her backpack over her shoulder, rushing from her room. She was going to be late to Bible study again. When she entered the kitchen where Jane and Roy were drinking coffee a few minutes earlier, she froze. Roy looked up. He had two pieces of paper laid out on the counter. He frowned at her.

"Put your bags down and take a look. Maybe you can explain what these papers are."

Neala slowly approached, glancing at her mother. Jane's face was white, and she was leaning against the refrigerator for support. Neala came to the counter and looked down at the two papers. Her heart skipped a beat. How? The Crusader poster and Trinity's Prayer-a-thon flyer stared Neala in the face. She glanced again at her mother as blood drained from her own face. Roy stood to his full height and placed his hands on his hips.

"Are you wondering how I found them? Well, I'll tell you. Last Friday, I came to surprise y'all with pizza and a movie, even got off work early. Nobody was home. I asked a neighbor and was told that for the past few weeks, my fiancée and her daughter have been going to a church function every night. I found that very interesting, especially after Jane promised me that she had pulled you out of Trinity." Roy shot Jane a condescending look. Neala balled her hands into fists. "So, what I'd like to know is how long this has been going on and whose idea it was?"

Neala felt his eyes on her now. She looked up to meet his smoldering glare. She tucked a piece of hair behind her ears. "You know it was my idea, Roy."

He took a step forward. "You know how I feel about God."

Neala closed her eyes. "Yes, Roy, I know how you feel about everything. Everyone knows how you feel about everything, especially God. Well, why did I go back to Trinity? Let me tell you." Neala took a deep breath. "For years I've been ignored and tossed aside. I thought that all there was to life was my mom's many boyfriends and a worldly point of view. I felt dirty from the inside out. Then…then I met Daniel Stevens, a boy with a faith like I've never encountered before. A boy whose faith helped him survive the pangs of an orphan heart while helping the helpless, witnessing to the lost, giving up his dreams for Christ's sake, and praying when the world told him not to. He showed me that maybe God did care for me. So I had to go back. I wanted to find God. Instead, He found me. I shared that joy with mom, and she's been coming with me to church. I'm a Christian now, Roy, and nothing you do can stop me from attending Trinity."

Roy sneered. "Daniel Stevens. I should have known." Roy shook his head. "That boy got what he deserved when Elliot beat him up." He pointed at Neala. "And that is exactly what you'll get if you keep going down this 'Christian' walk of yours. I swear, Neala, I will beat God out of you if I have to."

Neala took a step back. The flames of anger had been stoked in Roy's eyes, and it was something beyond Neala and Jane sneaking off to church. She crossed her arms. "Why do you hate God so much?"

"That is none of your business."

Jane, who had remained silent, spoke now, her voice shaking. "She has a right to know, Roy."

Roy spun on his heel and glared at her. Jane looked at him calmly, although Neala could read fear in her eyes. Finally, he sneered.

"Does she? Does she really?"

He fixed his eyes on her. The coldness in them made her shiver.

"Fine, if you want to know about your God, I'll tell you about Him." He looked around. "I used to live in an apartment like this. It was about this size actually. I was only five years old, and my father was a deacon in a local church." Neala raised her eyebrows. Roy laughed cynically in response. "Yeah, I wasn't always the demonic man you think me to be." Roy shot Jane a look of disgust. "We lived in that apartment until I was ten years old; and every Sunday we went to church as a family, me, my mom, and my dad. Sounds like a typical Georgian tale, right? Man, I even went to a Christian school. I was so sure that God had everything in control." Roy began pacing. "Then, one day, my dad got back late from Saturday visitation, the stupidest form of evangelism I've ever heard of. As he was getting out of his car, some gangsters jumped him." Roy frowned. "My dad had nothing on him. He had spent it all helping some needy family from the church. I watched from my window…in horror…as they gunned down my dad in cold blood."

Neala winced. She saw the pain in Roy's eyes, and all of the hatred she'd felt for him began to melt away. Jane sniffled beside her. Roy stepped closer and held up the prayer flyer from Trinity.

"You know what I did? I ran outside, sat in my father's pool of blood, and prayed. I prayed until my throat was so sore that I could barely speak. When I finally opened my eyes, he was already dead. And in his hands, he was holding a tract, running red with his own blood."

Roy ripped the prayer flyer in half and threw it at Neala's feet. "He was going to hand those good-for-nothings a blood-stained tract!" He spat on the shreds of paper and pointed a finger in Neala's face. "There is no power in prayer! It's nothing. We moved from that apartment; and I never looked back, not at the apartment, or the church, or the bloody tract, or the God Who let my father die in the parking lot of his own home. So, if you want me to continue to live civilly with the both of you, do not go back to Trinity. I'm trying to save you from disappointment."

Neala looked at the prayer flyer on the ground. Her heart ached because of Roy's story. She looked up at him, tears filling her eyes. "Even if we stopped going to Trinity again, I would never stop praising the God that I serve. I'm His now, Roy. I've been His for two months. I don't need you to save me from disappointment because Jesus already has saved me from sin. I'm not lost in religion, Roy; I'm found in Christ." She reached out and gently touched his shaking hands. "And I'm praying for you always. I didn't know you were so lost; but now that I do, I know what to pray for. The only way you can ever learn the reason behind this pain is if you let God take it, or so I've read in the Bible. I believe you will find your way back to Him, Roy."

"Do you really?" Roy pulled away and slapped Neala across the face. She gasped as the fire of his touch covered her cheek. Blinking, she stepped back and covered the handprint that marked her skin.

"That is what I think of your God and your precious Daniel and your Bible study and your prayers. On May 6, Trinity and the God that it stands for will fail, and you can do nothing to stop it. Your God is like that blood-stained tract. It's useless."

For a moment, Jane and Neala just stared. Then, Jane rose to her feet. She came to stand next to Neala and pulled her back protectively. Her eyes filled with tears. Neala could feel her trembling as she faced Roy.

"Get out," she whispered. "If you can't respect the God that my daughter loves, the God, might I add, whose people have helped me, I don't want you to step another foot into this house."

He guffawed. "Oh yeah? And who is going to pay your bills, Jane O'Malley?"

Jane tightened her hold around Neala. Neala looked at Roy and answered for her, even though her voice shook from the sting of Roy's slap. "God will."

Roy cursed at the response. Neala and Jane stood in the living room, clinging to each other as he stormed through the house to collect all the items he'd ever given Jane. By the time he was done, the sting of his slap had faded, but a fear for Daniel and Trinity rose in Neala's heart.

Roy swept past Jane and Neala without a second glance. On his way out the door, he shouted a string of curses back at them. Then, all was silent.

197

Neala helped her mother to the nearest couch. When she was settled, she sat next to her and fished out her cell phone. She dialed Daniel's number, waiting, with her heart in her throat. When he answered, she battled tears.

"Daniel, it's me, Neala."

"What's up? We haven't started our prayer group yet. Are you on your way?"

She bit her lower lip. "I'm there now." She sighed. "Look, I'm not going to make it physically this morning. Can you put me on speaker phone?"

Daniel paused, doing as she had asked. When he spoke again, his voice did not sound as close. "What's wrong? We're listening."

She smiled. He was always listening. Taking a deep breath, she recounted her conversation with Reganne and confrontation with Roy. By the time she was done, there was utter and complete silence on the other end of the phone. Did Roy's attitude suddenly make as much sense to them as it did to her? He had fallen into deep pain and never risen again. She felt the slap across her cheek again and placed her trembling hand against it. The next words she spoke were the hardest words she'd ever spoken in her life.

"Can we pray for him right now?"

Neala felt her mother's eyes on her at those words. She looked up and caught the look of disbelief in Jane's eyes. She smiled weakly at her mother. Daniel's voice came through the phone.

"Yes, I'm ready."

Trying to forget the fear Roy had brought upon their household moments ago, Neala closed her eyes. The voice of all The Crusaders, rising one at a time to ask for Roy's healing, began to work on the sting of the scars he had brought to her mother and to her. She squeezed her eyes shut. She had to forgive him. A hand reached for Neala's, and she felt her mother slipping in beside her. Neala wiped an unbidden tear off of her red cheek. She had to forgive him, for Christ's sake… and for hers.

CHAPTER 27
ULTIMATUM

Roy walked into the gym. His eyes skimmed over the number of boys filling the bleachers as he walked to the center. He nodded. Twenty-one. Perfect. Today, he was going to put an end to nonsense and prove which boys were really serious about soccer. He stopped in front of the center bleachers, placed his hands behind his back, and looked up at the Conquerors. He cleared his throat when he had their attention.

"Are you all aware that May 6 is the final registration for State? Coach Mackenzie informed me yesterday that he has filled out all of the paperwork and is ready to send it off in the morning. However, before that, I want a pledge from all of the team members here. It is a pledge that will seal your permanence as a Conqueror and your loyalty to the team."

Roy lifted up the Trinity prayer-a-thon flyer he had found in Jane's bedroom. His fingers burned just touching it. God had taken everything from him again, but this time Roy was ready to retaliate. He allowed all eyes to scan the page before speaking again.

"There have been rumors that many of our Conquerors have been attending Trinity's revival services. Now, what you do on your personal time is your business. However, what you do on May 6 is my business. We are going to represent Chancellor at State, and no part of Chancellor is symbolized by religion. I want each of you to make a

199

conscious decision today about choosing between this church's prayer-a-thon or going to State. If you are wise and choose State, you are not allowed to attend the prayer-a-thon. Those of you who do not show up at school on May 6 because of the prayer-a-thon will be crossed off of the player list before it is sent out in the mail. I think I've made myself clear."

At first, no one responded. They sat stoically, each individual contemplating the terms. Principal Wilkins smiled. Now the spirit of Trinity's revival would fall. These boys had trained too hard to throw it all away now. There was only one Daniel in a million other players. The rest would submit.

He lowered the prayer-a-thon flyer to the table behind him where Coach Mackenzie sat with the mailing folder. He got ready to draw a conclusion to the impromptu meeting. Before he could, however, Art stood. He walked toward him.

Wordlessly, he removed his jersey, placed it next to the prayer-a-thon poster, and walked toward the locker room. Then, one by one, boys who Roy had coached not long ago, walked away from the dream he'd handed them. In a matter of minutes, only five players were left sitting on the bleachers.

Coach Mackenzie hesitated, glancing at the pile of jerseys in front of him. Pushing back his chair, he brought Principal Wilkins the State papers. He laid them, along with the coach's whistle, atop the pile of jerseys. Principal Wilkins pounded his fist on the table.

"Mackenzie! Show some sense, Man. Drag those boys back in here."

Mackenzie shook his head. "I'd rather not be the one trying to stop God's work. I'm going to stand with Him."

Rage welled up in Wilkins as he watched Mackenzie walk away. He cursed under his breath, while staring into the malice-filled eyes of the five remaining players. The glint in Elliot's eyes sent danger signs blaring in his head. When someone else's dreams were crushed by others, the results could be catastrophic. Should he say something to reassure them that he would fix things? He shook his head. He needed sleep. Instead of pacifying his loyal Conquerors, he grabbed his briefcase. He left the jerseys and the last team members to their own devices.

†

The room was bursting with Trinity church members. They talked amongst themselves, sharing stories and happenings of the day. In a corner, Neala and Daniel listened intently as Art, Sean, Matthew, and Randy, surrounded by Garcia and recent Conqueror converts, told them about that afternoon's soccer practice.

"I didn't expect half of the soccer team to get up and leave," said Art.

"Neither did Principal Wilkins or Coach Mackenzie," Sean added.

"But that's not the best part," said Matthew, "Coach Mackenzie ran after us and asked us to lead him to salvation. I was so excited. He said that when he was younger he went to church but got lost in his ambitions in high school and never once gave it a second thought."

"That is, until he witnessed many soccer miracles after Daniel's arrival to Chancellor and more recently in the team as a whole since the revival," said Randy. He gave Daniel a sideways glance. "The prayer notes left on his desk helped a lot too."

Daniel scratched his chin. He cocked his head. "So, this would have been around four, right?"

Art nodded. "Same as always."

He laughed. "Unbelievable. That was exactly the time I was praying for you guys."

Neala smiled but said nothing in response. He sent her a questioning glance. She shook her head and shrugged. Before he could wonder any further, Pastor Moore walked into the room and called for silence. The people quieted instantly. The forty-eight hour mark had come. It was almost time. Pastor Moore smiled at his congregation.

"Thank you so much for gathering faithfully every day in preparation for the prayer-a-thon. Today's meeting is going to be short. On May 6, two days from now, we are going to host the prayer-

201

a-thon. I'm holding each of you responsible for the folder of prayer requests you were assigned. Until May 6, don't stop praying. We are expecting miracles and God's hand in all matters. Stay organized and focused. Members of Trinity Baptist Church, let's function in such a way on May 6 that the people in our area will say, as the Romans said of the Apostles, "These, who have turned the world upside down, have come."

The congregation asked a few more questions about the prayer-a-thon. Daniel kept Neala in his sights the whole time. She continuously kept glancing behind her. She looked nervous as he had never seen her since she got saved two months ago. When they bowed their heads in prayer, he said a special prayer for whatever was bothering Neala.

As the crowd began to thin, Daniel looked for Neala. He saw her heading out of Trinity's double doors. He made his way toward her.

"Neala!"

She turned at the sound of his voice. She smiled softly as he approached her. That was the biggest change in Neala since she got saved. She had a different smile. Daniel stopped beside her.

"Can I walk you to your car?"

She nodded. "Sure, if you don't mind carrying my flyer folder. My hands are kind of full with my music books."

"I can see that." He reached for the top of the pile and opened the door for her. They stepped out in the fading light and walked in silence for a few minutes. Neala's brow furrowed with whatever troublesome thoughts had been plaguing her all night. Daniel glanced at her.

"What's wrong?"

She purposely smoothed her brow. She opened her mouth, paused, then closed her mouth again. She shook her head. "I was going to say nothing but...I think I don't want to lie." She slowed her approach to her car. With a sigh, she pushed her hair out of her face and held it at the back of her head. "I'm just thinking a lot about Roy."

"Ah, I see. Has he been bothering you and your mother again?

She shook her head. "No, and that's the thing. It almost seems as if he's completely ignoring us and that doesn't sound like Roy. After what I heard today, I know he's still planning something." She bit her lower lip. "Then there's Elliot. He's been so hostile in his messages to me lately. It's kind of scaring me. It makes me worry..." Her voice faded as she dropped her gaze to the ground.

Daniel shielded his eyes against the lowering sun. "So, you're worried that they might ruin the prayer-a-thon. Neala, God's got this."

"I know, it's just, I'm not sure what Elliot and Roy are capable of."

Daniel sighed. He shrugged. "They're men, Neala. We have God on our side." They stopped in front of Neala's car. Her mother was already waiting for her inside. Daniel grinned and handed Neala her folder and Bible. "So, I'll see you tomorrow?"

She nodded. "This is one day I'm not going to miss. And, on May 6, all of your prayers are going to come to a peak. Right, Prayer Warrior? "

He froze. She knew? She shrugged and then placed a finger to her lips. Daniel winked. "Just remember..."

"I know, I know...it's not you. It's God."

As Neala and her mother drove out of the parking lot, Daniel glanced at the church sign. This week's quote said: ASAP: Always Say a Prayer. Join Trinity for a prayer-a-thon on the National Day of Prayer: Altar open all day long.

Daniel looked at Chancellor High. If May 6 came, it would not, could not, be him. It would be God.

†

He pressed against the shadows as the jeep drove into the parking lot. He held his breath, waiting for the passengers to climb out of the car. What were they doing here? It was going to ruin his plans. He looked over his shoulder to see three boys get out of the car. He smiled when he recognized them.

Actually, this was perfect. Maybe Daniel was with them. That would be a stroke of pure luck, for him this time. He waited until they were inside. Then, he pulled his hoodie around his face and approached the front of Trinity's church steps. He walked up them stealthily. Once he was at the front door, he grabbed a stack of sticky notes out of his pocket, leaving only one for later. He smirked.

Try to stop me, God.

He pulled a lighter from his other pocket. He allowed one small flame to lick the edges of the sticky note. Then, he placed his prayers from the anonymous prayer warrior at the foot of Trinity's wooden door. The flames immediately began to lick the base of Trinity's entrance. He smirked, pulled his hood even closer, and swiftly ran toward the church's sign.

Before running out into the dark street, he placed the last sticky note on the edge of the sign's brick base. The sound of flames fanned his hatred for this God and all who stood for Him. They had taken his dreams.

"You were warned, Daniel," he whispered into the night. "You were warned."

CHAPTER 28
FLAMES

"Daniel! Daniel, wake up!"

Daniel groaned. He tried to shake off his uncle's strong grip and turn over to catch a few more moments of sleep. His uncle shook him again, this time harder. Daniel groaned and pushed back the covers.

He rubbed his eyes. "What is it?"

Uncle Devon backed away, his eyes wide open. "I just got a call from Pastor Moore. Trinity is on fire!"

Daniel blinked in the darkness. Was this some kind of nightmare?

Uncle Devon called over his shoulder. "I'm heading on over there."

Daniel jumped out of bed. Before his uncle even left, he was reaching for his clothes. Once he was dressed, he noticed his cell phone blinking with a message. He picked it up, his hands trembling as he scrolled down to read the message. It was from Art.

Daniel,
We're meeting at Trinity for Bible study. We want to pray over the church before the prayer-a-thon tomorrow. See you there.

Daniel frantically glanced at the time on his cell phone. It was five o'clock. Art was always a half hour early. He shook his head. No, not Art! He rushed out of his room.

"Uncle Devon!" he screamed. "We have to leave now!"

God, deliver my friends.

†

Neala walked into the living room. Morning light filtered through the room, revealing a collection of dust mites floating in the air. "Mom?"

She frowned. The TV was still blaring the news channel she'd left it on while waiting for her mom to get back from the night shift. She sighed. They must have extended her hours again. The extra shifts were taking their toll on Jane but they weren't half as taxing as her emotional connection to Roy had been. Neala sighed, reaching for the remote control on the couch's arm rest. It was her turn to make breakfast again. Just as she was about to push the power button, the reporter's voice made her stop.

"Happening right now, a small community church has burst into flames. Trinity Baptist Church, located in front of Chancellor High School, caught fire this morning. There is no report on whether anyone was inside. Classes will be delayed at Chancellor High until the area is deemed safe by firefighters."

The reporter's voice faded. Neala stared at the screen as footage of Trinity's burning building flashed across her vision. *The Bible study!* Art had invited them all to meet at the church early to pray for the Prayer-a-thon. Had they been there when the fire started? *Daniel!*

Neala dropped the remote, rushing to her room. She dove for her cell phone on her dresser drawer. She had to get there now! Unlocking her screen, she began dialing her mom's number. Before she pressed the first digit, an incoming call flashed across the screen. Mom? She hit the answer button, snatching up her set of house keys, and heading toward the door.

"Hello, Mom? I was just going to call you. I'm heading to the

206

church right away. I'm sorry I couldn't make breakfast, but Trinity is on fire…"

"Neala?"

Neala froze, her hand on the doorknob. The voice on the other end was female but scratchy and tired. "Hello?"

"Neala? Hi, this is Shari from the office. I carpool sometimes with your mom."

She nodded slowly. "Okay…yeah, she's talked about you. Listen, is my mom with you? I need to…"

"No, Honey, see, that's why I'm calling. It's about your mom. She's in the emergency room."

Neala froze. "The emergency room?"

"Her old boyfriend came by and they were arguing. She was in bad shape when she left. I told her to let me drive her home, but she wouldn't. She's been in a car accident."

The words hit her like a blow to the head. She gasped, the room around her spinning. Shari was talking on the other end of the line, but she didn't hear her completely. Words like "still alive" and "not much information" made her heart sink further. Pinpricks of light mixed around her like stars. Her legs felt like jelly. She was falling. *Breathe!*

Neala took a deep breath, her vision coming back in a matter of seconds. She was still clinging to the doorknob but was barely standing. The door was holding all her weight. She took a few more breaths, slowing her heart rate.

"Neala?"

Tears clouded her vision. She gripped the sides of her phone. "I'm here."

"Do you have a way to get to the hospital?"

She rubbed her forehead, closing her eyes. "I don't know…I'm not…mom has the only car."

"Ok Honey, I'm already halfway to your house. Hang tight and I'll be there in ten minutes."

Neala sunk to the ground, forcing herself to take breath after breath. Why was this happening? She couldn't lose her mom, not after they'd come so far. The sound of sirens wailed in the distance. She placed her head on her knees, waiting, praying, and hoping for the best in a day that had turned into the worst.

†

By the time Daniel and his uncle arrived at the church, it was engulfed in flames. Smoke pervaded the area. Daniel covered his mouth in shock and protection. The fire trucks came only a few minutes behind them. He searched the perimeter and froze when he saw Art's jeep parked on the left side of the building. His heart leapt to his throat. He approached the car, intense heat rolling against his skin as he got closer. The car was empty.

Not them Father, not them.

He ran toward the building and got as close as he dare. Waves of heat already had set off the alarm. Daniel squinted, searching for an open window.

"Art! Sean! Matthew!"

Daniel felt his throat close. If they were in there, he might never see them again. He shielded his eyes as sparks flew toward him. "Art!"

"Daniel?"

Daniel wheeled around. Three figures came toward him from the direction of Trinity's back entrance. He inhaled his first sooty breath since arriving at the church. He rushed forward to meet his friends.

"Thank God," he said, taking a moment to embrace them. They didn't even have soot on their clothes. "I thought I'd lost y'all."

Art shook his head. "Sean forgot his Bible in the car. We stepped outside just when the alarm went off. When we realized what was happening, we called 9-1-1."

The flames burst through the Bible study room and sent glass shattering across Art's jeep. All four boys jumped back, fell to the ground, and rolled out of reach of the angry flames. Daniel felt strong arms lift him to his feet and lead him safely away from the fire.

"Let the fire fighters handle it, Daniel."

Daniel was genuinely relieved to hear Uncle Devon's voice. He spotted his friends recounting to an officer all they had just told him.

"Sounds as if you boys had a guardian angel watching over you."

Daniel smiled. As the flames broke through the roof, he rushed toward one of the fire trucks. He was going to help them save Trinity any way he could. From the corner of his eye, he noticed something blowing on the side of the church sign. He walked over to it. A small green sticky note stuck to the edge of the sign's brick foundation. Daniel peeled off the sticky note. His hairs stood on end. Over the top of his usual prayer message, large bold letters had been printed.

I HATE YOU.

Daniel swallowed hard and gazed at Trinity. All at once, he understood. His enemies were throwing God's people into the furnace. Daniel closed his eyes. Was God in the midst of these flames?

†

"Miss Baptiste?"

Neala pulled away from the television news and drew her attention to the nurse. Her thoughts still whirled in disbelief. The most recent newscast reported no fatalities in Trinity's fire, but Chancellor's classes would not resume until tomorrow. Neala stood and walked toward the nurse. The elderly woman's eyes told Neala that this battle had ended as well. The nurse smiled gently.

"Your mother is resting. She suffered numerous broken ribs and a blow to the head, but she's going to pull through. You're welcome to stay here until she wakes up."

Neala looked around the empty waiting room. "Can I sit with her?"

The nurse nodded. "Of course."

The nurse walked Neala down the sterile hallway. Why did hospitals have to be so cold? The nurse stopped in front of Room 311. Neala took a deep breath and reached for the door handle.

"Sweetheart," said the nurse, "would you like us to notify anyone else?"

Neala shook her head. "No, that won't be necessary. It's just us. Thank you."

Inside, the room was dark and cool. Her mother lay on a bed, swathed in clean white sheets and a woolen blanket. She was sleeping peacefully, her head wrapped in bandages and scratches. Neala's heart ached at the sight. This darkened room cast her mother's face in shadows. Neala wiped away tears from her cheek. Why was she always crying? When was the last time she had laughed? When was the last time she felt joy instead of pain?

At the altar...Amazing Grace.

Neala's eyes widened. She lowered herself into the chair near her mother's bedside. It was so hard to pray for God's will. How could this be something good?

Pray.

Neala looked around, expecting to see Daniel standing in the room. It sounded like something he might whisper to her in this moment. She looked out the window at the rising sun. A small ray fell on her hands, and she stared at it.

No, this wasn't Daniel speaking. He was fighting Trinity's flames. This was the Solicitor of Amazing Grace. Neala took a deep breath. She glanced at her mother. There was still something she could do for her. Neala closed her eyes. She clasped her strong hands and used them to plead for peace and assurance. God might still use this as a final note in Jane's symphony.

†

Daniel coughed to clear his lungs. The perimeter was covered in soot and ashes. He shook hands with another firefighter. Then, he walked toward Pastor Moore. The preacher spoke with the fire chief, shaking his head and nodding. The elderly man's shoulders drooped. As Daniel came up behind them, Pastor Moore reached out and shook the fire chief's hand.

"Thank you for your help. We will certainly follow your precautions."

Pastor Moore turned to face Daniel. He smiled slightly and placed his arm over his shoulders. They both gazed at the pile of ashes and small frame that used to be Trinity. Pastor Moore sighed. "It's not good, Son. I think our revival services ended just on time." He took a deep breath.

"Daniel, the firefighter doesn't think we should meet here tomorrow. Based on the note you showed us, it is obvious that this church is being targeted for violence. We don't want any of the members to get hurt." Pastor Moore scratched his chin. "I'm sending out a memo of my own. We have to cancel the prayer-a-thon."

Daniel took a deep breath. He looked at the ashes. So, the people of God were giving in. The revival had not lasted very long. He moved away from Pastor Moore. He might gain some leverage on this issue if he called Mr. Pierce, but he doubted much would change. The lions of the world had ignited this furnace, and they would not stop until the congregation was nothing but ashes.

Daniel knelt down in a pile of ashes. The metal cross that had hung over the baptistry and shadowed Trinity's altar lay before him, black, with smoke rising from its body. He glanced upward. Who could hate his God so much?

Daniel pressed his palms against the ashes. Somewhere in there lay the altar which he had seen hold the tide and surge of revival. Now, it would remain empty. What could he do without the church? He glanced back at the sky. The building might be gone, but Satan still had the church body to reckon with. He stood on Trinity's black ground, refined by fire. He inclined his head toward the cross and then turned.

Tomorrow was the National Day of Prayer. Even if everyone else tried to stop it, one person would be praying. If the body of Christ refused to go through with the prayer-a-thon, then Daniel purposed in his heart that he would observe it. Tomorrow, he would stand and call on the name of the Lord for God's people.

CHAPTER 29
ASHES

Before dawn, Daniel stepped into the ashes of Trinity Baptist Church. The streetlights still shone against a dark sky. His legs trembled from the long walk to the church site. They trembled even more when he arrived. The pile of ashes was desolate. No one had come after all. Daniel took a deep breath. He knelt in the ashes, getting soot all over his jeans but not really caring. He bowed his head. He had to believe that, somewhere, the members were observing the National Day of Prayer. He could not give up hope now.

He lifted a pile of prayer requests from the folder he'd been given at the beginning of Trinity's prayer-a-thon planning. He laid them out before him, on sacred ground, where the altar would have been had the flames not come. The National Day of Prayer had begun.

†

Daniel interrupted Neala's dreams in a whisper.

I'll see you at Trinity on May 6…May 6.

Neala's eyes flew open. Her eyes searched the walls for a calendar. Today was May 6! She got ready to jump out of bed, but the movement sent pain through her sore muscles. She groaned, blinking in the dim light. The surroundings of her mother's hospital room came into focus. She glanced at her mother, sleeping soundly in the hospital bed. Everything from the night before came back to her. She closed her eyes. It was May 6, but Trinity was no longer standing. Should she call Daniel?

"Neala?"

Neala opened her eyes at the sound of her mother's voice. She rushed over to her side. "Mom? I thought you were still sleeping."

Jane shook her head. She sighed and looked up at the ceiling. "Just shutting my eyes against the pain."

She swallowed hard. She squeezed her mother's hand and nodded. "Do you need the nurse?"

She shook her head, stroking her daughter's hand. A small tear made its way from the corner of Jane's eyes to the back of her ear. Jane took a deep breath. "I have everything I need right here.:

Neala laid her head against the white sheets. Her mother sighed, her chest rising and falling evenly. "Except for maybe one thing."

Jane caressed her daughter's fingers. "I was so afraid in that moment of the accident. I thought I was going to die, and I remember thinking that I'd never see you again. I remember thinking I wasn't ready to die. So, I talked to God. I told Him I want to live." She squeezed her eyes shut. "But just living is not enough. I have to live differently... like my Neala." Neala leaned forward as her mother continued. "Neala, God has changed you, hasn't He?"

Neala nodded, her throat constricting. Jane smiled, the visible lines under her bandage smoothing over. "So, that's the deal I made with God. I told Him if He'd let me live, I'd let Him change me like He's change you. The thing is, I don't really know where to start."

Neala closed her eyes in wonder. Was this really happening? She smiled. "You're off to a good start. It's all about talking to Him. Just talk to Him, Mom."

"Will you...will you pray with me, Neala?"

She squeezed her mother's hand and bowed her head against Jane's wrist. She could not begin right away. Her tears clogged up her throat. Finally, she swallowed and took a shaky breath.

"Dear God and Saviour..."

Neala had to say no more. Before she could continue, her mother's voice rose up in prayer.

"God, I know I am the least of these, and I don't deserve Your care or Calvary's sacrifice about which Pastor Moore preaches every week. However, I know that You have given me a second chance. I need You to care for me and hold me in Your hands. Make me a new creation, like the one I've seen in my daughter, Neala. Reserve a place for me in Heaven and teach me Your ways. I'm done trying to survive on my own. I'm Yours now."

Jane finished her prayer in a sob. Neala joined her, and they clung to each other for the next few minutes, in joy instead of fear and triumph instead of battle. Jane whispered against Neala's hair.

"The emptiness is gone."

Neala smiled. "That's one of the best parts about God."

After a few more minutes, the tears had ceased. Mother and daughter clung to each other, smiling and breathing in unison. God had done so much more than save the hearts of two sinners. He had mended a broken family. Jane sighed and kissed the top of Neala's head.

"Sweetheart," she whispered, "isn't today May 6?"

She sighed. "Trinity burnt down, Mother. I don't think the prayer-a-thon is going to happen."

Jane was silent for a few moments. Then, she shook her head. "Just because of a few flames?" Jane laughed softly. "I don't think flames of any sort are going to stop Daniel...or God. You promised him you would be there, Neala."

"I'm already late."

"Hmmm, it's a good thing God doesn't put that label on time."

Neala tipped her face upward. She gazed into her mother's gleaming eyes. She smiled when she saw it. God's peace was a part of her now. Jane brushed back a stray strand of Neala's hair.

"Go, Neala. Go join your prayer warrior. I'll be praying for everyone right here."

She didn't hesitate another instant. She eased off of the bed, grabbed her purse lying near the chair she'd slept in, and walked toward

215

the door. Today was the National Day of Prayer. Whether Trinity's building stood or not, the people of God would. Before leaving, she looked back at her mother.

"I love you, Mom," she said.

Jane blinked back more tears. "I love you too, Neala."

Neala grinned. She closed the door behind her and walked down the hallway with a spring in her step. Every day, she was learning something new about Who her God was.

†

Daniel furrowed his brow. He heard footsteps, thousands of footsteps coming down the sidewalk. He shifted on his knees. How many more distractions could he stand? He closed his eyes more tightly.

In the midst of his prayer, he felt a slight breeze beside him. The ashes all around him shifted at different intervals. He heard the sound of whispers, gentle yet fervent, joining his. He paused. Curious, he opened his eyes. His eyes widened in shock at the sight of hundreds of pairs of shoes filling the perimeter. He lifted his head.

The footsteps took the form of hundreds of people. Daniel gaped as, one by one, students from Chancellor High took a step across the walkway dividing them from Trinity and stepped into the ashes. To the left, in the direction of the parking lot, church members approached the site of their ruined building. They formed a circle around Daniel, the body of Christ assembling where there was no place of comfort.

One by one, they took out their folders and began to pray. Daniel felt tears come to his eyes as students from Chancellor withdrew hundreds of sticky, prayer notes from their pockets and stuck them to the edge of Trinity's church sign.

Pastor Moore stood by the sign, his Bible in hand. As each student stopped with a prayer note, he asked, "Do you know Christ?"

Daniel took deep breaths, but nothing could calm the sobs that rose from within him. All of the labor in prayer that he had put in was culminating. The revival had lasted.

As sobs began to wrack his body, he felt a hand resting on his shoulder. He looked up. Neala smiled down at him and slipped to her knees. She laid out her prayer folder beside his and bowed her head. Daniel followed suit, but he found no words to thank God enough. So, instead, for the next few hours as other voices rose, Daniel thanked God with his unutterable prayers.

Around noon, the prayer-a-thon came to an end. Daniel opened his eyes, his heart and mind full of praise. One by one, people stood from the ashes and formed a circle. Daniel stood with them. Beside him, Neala reached for his hand. Giving it a squeeze, she faced the American flag across the street on Chancellor's flagpole. Her voice rose in sweet melody.

"God bless America, land that I love, stand beside her and guide her through the night with a light from above..."

All around Trinity's remains, people lifted their voices in song, asking for one last blessing over their nation. Daniel's voice was shaky as he joined them. The flames had not stopped them. Together, they stood.

CHAPTER 30
REMNANT

Roy walked proudly down the silent hallways. It had been noiseless all morning, peaceful, just as it should be in the midst of academic studies. This was the epitome of his plans. This tranquil place with no chaos. He smiled. So, May 6 had come just as it had every year before with absolutely no difference.

He stopped in front of Chancellor's front doors and gazed at the full parking lot. His students had arrived, and God had not. Things were just as they should be.

Resuming his walk through the hallways, he spotted the Chemistry room. Ah yes, they had done one of his favorite labs this morning. Principal Wilkins walked into the lab room and found it... empty?

Roy glanced at the wall clock. It was almost noon; fourth hour should be well under way. Not even Professor Rodney sat in his usual place. He backed out of the room. He continued down the hallway, opening each classroom door and finding the same results. None of this made sense. Where were his students? He walked quickly toward the front office. His secretary looked up when he walked in. Principal Wilkins spoke before she could say her usual, "Good morning."

"Did anyone check in this morning?"

The secretary looked at her computer screen. "Elliot and Hank stopped by a few minutes ago asking the same thing. No one else has come by, not even the staff."

Roy gripped the edge of the office counter. "Did you send the memo about Chancellor resuming classes today?"

The secretary nodded. She narrowed her eyes. "You know, it is May 6."

The blood drained from Principal Wilkins's face. He walked out of the office. Trinity was no longer standing. He had seen the memo about the cancellation of the prayer-a-thon with his own eyes. He burst out the front doors of Chancellor High and began walking across the parking lot. His heart raced as he got closer and closer to the walkway separating Chancellor and Trinity. About a dozen of his missing students already stood at the crossroads. As he drew nearer, he heard the sound of voices. He froze next to Elliot, Hank, and a handful of other students.

A few feet away, standing in a circle atop the ashes of Trinity, were more than half of Chancellor's students. They held hands, hundreds of voices singing "God Bless America."

Roy stared in wonder. Their church had fallen. He had done everything he could to end the spirit of revival among the students. Someone else had started a fire to stop them. There was nothing left of Trinity but ashes!

He gazed at those on top of the ashes. He felt faint. No, there was much more left of Trinity. The body of Christ was still there. Did that mean God was too? He thought of the prayer notes he had received recently, the ones he had thrown in the recycle bin. He thought of the boys giving up their soccer dreams and his father lying in a pool of blood, for the sake of "religion." Perhaps it wasn't religion. Religion alone wasn't strong enough for someone to die for. He could separate church and state, but would he ever separate God and state? The thought left him breathless.

Those across the street at Trinity began a new refrain of "God Bless America." Principal Wilkins looked at the flag fluttering above him. The red, white, and blue emblem of the nation danced in the wind, pointing directly toward Trinity. He shook his head. Slowly, he backed away and began to turn.

"Principal Wilkins!"

He paused. Behind him, Elliot stood with his arms folded across his chest. He frowned and pointed at Trinity. "Aren't you going to stop them?"

Roy shook his head. "I have no right to."

Elliot's mouth hung open. "So, you are just going to let them pray together? After all we've done to stop them?"

We? He raised his eyebrows, making Elliot shift from one foot to another. Principal Wilkins bit his lower lip, his eyes falling on the Trinity prayer-a-thon again. He sighed, scratching the back of his head. "Elliot, this is a free country. I think it's time we stop messing with freedom. Besides, I don't think this is about us."

Elliot frowned. "What do you mean?"

He pointed toward Trinity. "Figure it out."

Roy walked back to Chancellor and rushed into his office. He leaned against the wooden door for support. *I don't think this is about us.* He shook his head and began to pace.

When the students finally filed into Chancellor High and the afternoon classes resumed, he tried to forget the song, the flag, and the prayer-a-thon. He filed papers and took parent's calls. He signed detention slips, typed financial reports, and interviewed students for next year's enrollments. The entire time, the image of Chancellor's students crossing over into Trinity and praising God stayed on his mind.

When the dismissal bell rang, he immediately began packing up for the day. He had to get home. He had to sleep and get rid of this headache. As he shut the light off in his office and made his way to exit the main office, the secretary handed him an envelope.

"What's this?" he asked.

The secretary shrugged. "Garcia dropped it off for you."

Roy nodded. Without another word, he exited Chancellor and rushed to his car. Once he was inside, he took the first real breath all day. He laid his briefcase in the passenger's seat. With a sigh, he opened the envelope Garcia had dropped off and reached inside. His hands grabbed hold of...sticky notes? Roy pulled out a pile. In different forms of penmanship, some sloppy others neat, two hundred sticky notes had the same message on them.

I'm praying for you.

Roy could only stare at the notes. The revival had lasted. These notes were a testament. Even after the flames, prayer continued. With shaky hands, he rammed his key into the ignition. Trembling, he drove home, his heart in his throat. He needed to sleep this off.

That night, Roy lay alone in his bedroom. He stared at the television. On top of the big screen lay an envelope full of sticky notes from Chancellor students. He played with the remote, trying to decide which channel would best distract him. He had no desire to watch sports or an action film tonight. He stretched and glanced at his bottom dresser drawer. He took a deep breath. Slowly, he lifted himself from the edge of the bed and crossed the room.

His hands trembled as he opened the drawer. Pushing aside his enormous pile of ties, he reached down and grabbed a small piece of folded paper. The face of the paper was still smudged with his father's blood. He had tried to wipe it all away on the night of his father's death but stubborn smudges remained. He caressed the tract with his thumb. Could he really hate what his father had died for? Could he really fight against the God Who had allowed such enormous things to happen today? Was this God he'd been so against for most of his life the One Who had been in Trinity's ashes? Roy closed his eyes momentarily. Then, he pried open the blood-stained tract.

CHAPTER 31
ASSEMBLED

The students glanced at one another, questions in their eyes. The parents were joining them again today, the last Friday assembly of the year.

Art nudged Daniel in the side. "What's going on?"

Daniel shook his head. "I'm not really sure."

The boys quieted as they watched Neala walking toward them. Daniel smiled, his chest filling with pride, when the lights above him reflected off of his class ring now resting on her finger. She shot him a radiant smile. He sighed. God had given him more than he ever asked for. Reganne walked behind her, tucking her hair behind her ears, her eyes darting nervously between The Crusaders and those above them. Neala stopped before them.

"Daniel, Reganne was wondering if there is room for one more Crusader?"

He smiled at Reganne and fished a tract out of his pocket. "Anytime," he said, handing her the tract.

Reganne grabbed the tract but then frowned. "Don't try to convert me. I just want to see what the big deal is with you Christians."

Neala took a seat on the bleachers next to Daniel. She patted the empty spot beside her and smiled up at her lost friend. She answered Reganne with words similar to Daniel's thoughts. "God is."

When all of the students were seated, Principal Wilkins took the gym stage. Everyone else scurried to their seats. Daniel cocked his head. There was something different in the way Principal Wilkins took the stage. He paused, looking out over the crowd. Everyone glanced at each other in the awkward silence. Principal Wilkins gripped the edge of the podium.

"What I have to say today is difficult," he scratched his chin, "especially after everything that happened at the assembly at the beginning of the year. Principal Wilkins looked away from the audience. "I really just wanted to change one of my statements from the beginning of the year about my new policy. I said that The Crusaders Bible study was null and void and that no religious activity would be allowed on campus."

Daniel held his breath. All of The Crusaders glanced at one another, eyes wide.

"A few weeks ago, on May 6, I realized that, even if I did try to get rid of 'religion', there was no way I was going to get rid of God. And also, that I was infringing on the 'freedom of religion.' For this reason, starting next year, the Bible study and morning prayer will resume on the campus of Chancellor High."

Daniel gasped. Immediately, the students around them, those who had found Christ in the midst of Trinity's revival, stood to their feet and began to applaud. The entire gym reverberated with the praise of God's people as the ban was lifted. Daniel, Art, Sean, Matthew, and Randy embraced one another in pure joy. Principal Wilkins held up his hand for silence. Everyone sat down, smiles making their faces glow. Principal Wilkins cleared his throat.

"Thank you for joining me in this short meeting today." He looked up at The Crusaders. "May God bless and protect all of you this summer. You will all be in my…prayers."

The assembly was silent as Principal Wilkins walked off the stage. Art glanced at Daniel. Had Principal Wilkins just said he would be praying for them? Art winked, slid off the bleachers, and walked toward the stage stair where Principal Wilkins was. As he walked away, Daniel felt a strong arm grip his shoulder. He turned to find Elliot standing above him, his eyes as dark as ever before. He swallowed hard. Could they not keep peace during their last week of high school?

To his surprise, Elliot released him and stepped down one bleacher to stand beside him.

"Hey, Rookie, just so you know, I've got my eyes on you." He shrugged. "Maybe I'll go spy on your little Bible study next week."

Daniel swallowed hard. Was this his opening? He grinned. "Well, just so you know, Elliot, there is always room at the Bible study…and Trinity…for you."

He shrugged. He looked across the gym. "Maybe." He looked back at Daniel and nodded. "Maybe."

Elliot sighed and walked away, his gait just as cocky as it had been before. Daniel glanced around at the emptying gym. He caught sight of Art, on the far end, shaking Principal Wilkins's hand while Mr. Pierce smiled at the changed principal. His heart leapt for joy. He shifted his sights to those around him.

The faces of most of the students were glowing. Some of the parents still looked confused at this turn of events; but Daniel knew, without a doubt, that the parents would soon learn Who God was too. That was the next thing he had to pray for.

Beside him, Neala grabbed his hand and squeezed it. She smiled and mouthed "God Bless America." He squeezed her hand in return and smiled. Yes, God would bless America, and He would start here, in a little Georgia town. The gap between Chancellor and Trinity had been breached. This high school would defy the odds to bring Christ back. Daniel closed his eyes, took a deep breath, and then released it. Finally, God was here.

EPILOGUE

Daniel laid the roster on the ground beside him. Next to the roster, he laid a missionary card. Little feet stood beside his bent knees. He felt a small, warm hand resting on his thigh and turned to look into the face of his daughter. Her wide blue eyes gazed at the papers in front of her. She furrowed her little brow, just like her mother's, and her long black hair fell over her shoulders as she pointed to the items on the ground.

"This is wok?"

Daniel grinned. Her inquisitive nature was always a wonder to him. He reached for her hand and pulled her into his lap. He nodded against her hair.

"Yes, Bella, this is part of Daddy's work. Now, in a little while, a whole bunch of boys are going to run onto this field, and I'm going to teach them how to play soccer."

"Like Mommy!" said Bella, her little hands clapping.

Daniel smiled as he envisioned Neala and Bella running around with him in their backyard every afternoon. He nodded. "Yes, like with Mommy. This time, though, teaching them soccer is part of my job." He pushed back Bella's bangs and then pointed back at the roster and missionary card on the field. "But, there is a bigger part of my job. It's bigger than playing with my students."

"What?"

Daniel looked at the papers in front of him. "Prayer, Munchkin. Talking to God is a big part of Daddy's job. And yes, sometimes, it is very hard work." He paused and tucked a strand of stray hair behind her ear. She never ceased to look unruly. "Still, it's the best time in the world. Praying to God. Even when God and I fight, He shows me what's best. It's part of being God's soldier."

Bella gasped, her eyes lighting up. She grabbed a fistful of Daniel's sweatpants. "Oooh. Like Mommy's song. Are you a soldier?"

"More than you know."

Bella nodded. "Then I have to pway more to be a strong soldier for God." Bella paused suddenly and glanced around. She looked up at Daniel. "Is Uncle Arfur coming today?"

Daniel's eyes fell on the missionary card. Art and Maribel Falcon: Missionaries to Peru. Daniel shook his head. "No, your Uncle Art is playing on a different field today. That is why I have his card here. Today, we have to pray for extra safe travel for Uncle Art as he goes to share God's gift with other people."

Bella wrinkled her nose. "I don't like shawring. Can we just keep him?"

Daniel poked her dainty nose. She squirmed at the touch, making Daniel smile. "We have to share things all the time, and the most important thing we can share with others is God."

"Cuz He wuvs the whole werld." Bella opened her arms wide, almost smacking Daniel in the face, to make her point. "That's what Mommy says."

"That's right, Munchkin."

Bella looked back at the papers on the ground. "Is shawring God wok?"

Daniel nodded. "It's the most important part of my job. When I come here to pray, it helps make the job of teaching soccer and sharing God easier. One day, when you grow up and learn to love God as much as He loves you, then you will see that sharing God is the best kind of work."

Bella slid off of her father's lap. She tucked her feet under her, taking a position similar to Daniel's. She looked up at Daniel and grinned. "I still don't want to shawr Uncle Arfur."

Daniel sighed. "Me neither, Munchkin. Me neither."

The field was quiet without his assistant coach joining him in prayer. Daniel closed his eyes, trying to recapture the moments that had brought both he and Art back to Chancellor and led up to their coaching of the Conquerors. A chance encounter at the same college and a delayed missions' trip had given them the opportunity to work together with the Conquerors for two years.

Daniel was not playing professional soccer like Randy, but he had found a way to use soccer as a venue for the Gospel. Little by little, one day at a time, the gap between Chancellor and Trinity was getting smaller. He was privileged to be a part of it. Still, it was very quiet without Art.

His thoughts were interrupted by Bella's humming of "Jesus Loves the Little Children." Daniel smiled. Well, not really that quiet.

Bella stopped humming and Daniel opened his eyes. She was looking up at him, her eyes big. Those eyes had the same expressions as Neala's. She tugged on his whistle.

"Do you want me to stawt?"

Before Daniel could answer, Bella settled down onto her knees, placed her dress securely about her, bowed her head, and closed her eyes. Her sweet voice made Daniel's throat constrict.

"Dear God, this is Daddy's bestest guwrl Bella. Daddy says every day that You wuv me even mo' than he wuvs me. He says You are his fwiend. So, I want to say hi. Mommy says that Daddy is the bestest at pwraying. Now, Daddy has to wok. I'm jus' stawting."

Daniel closed his eyes. He rested his head against his daughter's hair and held her close. Yes, Bella would know God. One of these days, she would understand the colors of faith that Neala presented to her every week during Sunday school. One day, with enough prayer and guidance, Bella Jane Stevens would have her name written in the Book of Life. Hopefully, she would not be the last but, instead, one of the first in this new generation—just like Daniel had been, when his mother led him in his first prayer.

Daniel clasped Bella against him. Closing his eyes, he took a deep breath. "Dear God, this is Daniel."

There was no need to say more. As Daniel knelt there on Chancellor's soccer field, with his daughter beside him, God leaned down from His throne and listened.

ACKNOWLEDGEMENTS

There is no way I could thank all of those who had a part in the making of this book, but I would like to especially thank a few who made this dream a reality.

To my Lord and Saviour Jesus Christ: You gave me the gift of words and ignited this story in my heart. Every step I take is because of You. I hope this story honored You most of all.

To my pastor, Greg Neal: You took a chance on this story and expanded my vision of what God can do with a dream.

To the editing team of Berean Publications: You made this story readable and coherent.

To my husband: You are the one person I could not imagine going on this journey without. You have been my constant supporter and fan, and my knight in shining armor.

To my family: Your excitement about this project kept me going on the hardest days.

To my first readers, Emily Smith and Jessica Swanda: You both believed in this story even when it was just scribbled on a beat up old journal. Thanks for being fans from the start.

To my Word Weavers Critique Group: Your insights and suggestions have made me a better writer. I am so blessed to have found such an amazing group with which to work.

To the 2011 Senior Class of OSCS: You inspired so many people and themes in this book with your push for revival in our last year together. Never stop serving Christ!

And lastly, to every person that picks up this book: Thank you for taking a chance on this story. I hope Daniel's journey blesses your heart and refreshes your soul.

ABOUT THE AUTHOR

VIctoria Isabel Roberts

Victoria has been telling stories for as long as she can remember. In middle school, she learned the art of writing a novel and has been writing voraciously ever since. She likes to draw on experiences from working in the ministry to write about characters with bold faith in a broken world. When she is not writing, she enjoys reading various forms of fiction, working in ministries at her local church, or hanging out with her husband and spoiled toy poodle.

Follow her writing journey through these social media outlets:
Facebook: https://www.facebook.com/readywriter31/
Twitter: https://twitter.com/readywriter31
Instagram: @carpediem4christ

www.ingramcontent.com/pod-product-compliance
Lightning Source LLC
Chambersburg PA
CBHW061137170626
46809CB00003B/896